MW01098700

Heaven Only Knows

A sweet and sour story of love and murder

– DAVID MCLAREN –

An environmentally friendly book printed and bound in England by
www.printondemand-worldwide.com

Mixed Sources
Product group from well-managed
forests, and other controlled sources
www.fsc.org Cert no. TT-COC-002641
© 1996 Forest Stewardship Council
FSC

PEFC Certified
This product is
from sustainably
managed forests
and controlled
sources
PEFC
PEFC/16-33-415
www.pefc.org

This book is made entirely of chain-of-custody materials

www.fast-print.net/store.php

Heaven Only Knows
Copyright © David McLaren 2012

ISBN 978-178035-498-9

First published 2012 by
FASTPRINT PUBLISHING
Peterborough, England.
Printed by Printondemand-Worldwide

For my wonderful wife Arlette, our son David and his family, Lea and Mia, who tolerate my imperfections while understanding I love them without limit

David McLaren

Chapter One

"Granddad, may I ask you a question?"

How do you refuse a twelve-year-old lady? I replied, "You may, sweetheart."

Ellie asked with a mischievous grin, "Do you promise to tell the truth?"

We were sitting on empty sands, with arms around bent legs, watching the North Sea crashing into thunderous chaos and foam on the beach. Noisy gulls and silent cormorants dived into the water looking for food. The morning fog had lifted; the wind, usually as sharp as a butcher's knife, was subdued and a blue sky touched the far horizon. From a nearby fairground, loud carousel music pulsated over the sand dunes.

I responded, "I will never lie to you, sweet pea. Never have and I never will."

She turned her head of beautiful copper-red curls and looked at me. "Cross your heart and hope to die?"

3

Smiling, I replied, "Cross my heart and hope to die."

Ellie paused, finding some residue of confidence and asked slowly, "Does God actually exist?"

I shrugged. "Um, that's a tough question and the honest answer is I really don't know. Some people say they know, but the truth is you can only choose to believe. Nobody knows for sure."

It seemed only yesterday since Ellie was born. To her twelve years was a lifetime, while those dozen years were hardly two fingers on my eon glass.

My granddaughter gave me a slight smile, more childlike than juvenile. "Do you believe, Granddad?"

"I'll tell you what I do believe, sweetheart." I looked into Ellie's angel eyes and said, "I believe it's a marvel our planet finds itself in the precise place for life to exist. Earth is the perfect distance from the sun, not too hot and not too cold."

Ellie spluttered with enthusiasm, "Just like Goldilocks and the three bears." She produced a wide smile, a contagious grin that made me smile.

"Yes, just like Goldilocks' porridge, not too hot and not too cold, just right."

Ellie picked up a handful of sand and watched it escape through her fingers. When the last grain disappeared, she turned her head and looked at me. "What's that got to do with God?"

I shrugged my shoulders. "Well someone had to put it in the right place. They also had to tilt the planet so we can get our four seasons."

Ellie's eyes widened. "Did God tilt the earth, how did he do it?"

"A big rock came out of space and hit the planet, tilting it exactly the right way so we could have the seasons for plants to grow."

"So God did it?" Ellie's eyes widened.

"If he didn't it was very fortunate it happened, otherwise we and the animals couldn't have food and survive here."

"How do you know a big rock hit the earth?"

"Because the debris left over from the impact made the moon."

"Really?" Ellie sounded incredulous, her eyebrows coming together, unsure if it was one of her granddad's windups.

Putting on my best honest voice, I replied, "Yes, and without the moon we wouldn't have tides." I indicated towards the sea with my chin.

Ellie giggled. "You're being silly, the moon doesn't give us tides."

"It does, young lady, and I'll tell you something else. Do you know the moon is exactly the right distance from earth, so that when a lunar eclipse happens the moon fits *exactly* over the sun?" I made a circle with my left thumb and index finger and put my other fist some distance behind it, to illustrate. I continued, "It looks like it was designed to be spot on. If it was closer, it would be too big and further away it would be too small."

"Like Goldilocks again." Ellie ran her fingers through her thick hair.

She looked just like her mother did when she was this age. Images from a time long ago drifted through my mind: buckets of memories of playing on the sand and of fish and chips from Frank's café. Happy postcard memories, keepsakes locked away, safe in my mind.

"Yes, just like Goldilocks." I agreed.

"So does God exist?"

"I told you, I don't know." I paused again before announcing, "But I do KNOW what you are thinking." I tweaked her button nose and smiled.

Ellie asked in anticipation, "Well?"

I teased, "What?"

"What am I thinking?"

I announced confidently, "You're wondering if Granddad will walk you to the fair and BUY you an ice cream."

"Yes I am, you are so clever, Granddad! That's exactly what I'm thinking." Ellie jumped up, excitement lighting her face. "How did you know?"

"I know because I'm a clever granddad. Come on, let's get you a big ice cream and don't tell your mum." I paused a few seconds before asking, "Can you remember all those years ago when I told you what an echo was?" I stood up and brushed away the sand from my clothes. Holding hands, we started walking towards the fairground music. I felt the sand beneath my shoes, a few grains spilling into my brogues. Walking in her bare feet, Ellie carried her sandals as if they were made of delicate crystal.

Eventually, she announced with a happy voice, "Yes, you told me an echo is nature's instant reply."

I replied, "Well remembered, sweetheart."

We walked about a hundred yards, the music from the carousel getting louder when Ellie said, "My teacher, Mr Haines, once told us, even if you keep a seed for a hundred years and then add water and sun, the seed will grow into a plant. How does that work, Granddad?"

I didn't reply.

I had no more answers, my head slumped and my echo shattered like a dropped window pane. I was empty and deflated. With no more words for my gorgeous granddaughter, I couldn't explain how the seed germinates, the same way she had in her mother's womb. Didn't have the words to tell Ellie it was a miracle, just as all life is a miracle, and there must be a creator to make this planet with its seasons, its blue skies, white snow and green grass. Or how she was designed to give life some time in the future, to carry her own child and hold the baby to her breast or how special it would feel.

I stopped and looking behind I could see my trail of footprints, already degrading as the fine sand filled in the indent, disappearing from the landscape.

Nature hates a vacuum.

Ellie's footprints were not there. Her small feet had left no mark. I looked at my hand. There was no Ellie.

All I could see was my tight, angry fist with white knuckles.

Images of the funeral flooded my brain. It was only a few weeks but the raw pain returned, flaying my insides, cutting deep.

I could hear the gulls, more raucous. The horizon disappeared under a bank of storm clouds and the wind returned; cold and sharp.

I collapsed onto the sand like a puppet with cut strings. I sobbed as bitter tears of sadness and anger intermingled. The sound of my weeping faded on the wind as my mind drained away all thoughts save for the question that refused to go away.

If there was a God, how could he allow a twelve year old to die?

Chapter Two

*M*y name is Ellie Peach, like the fruit and my granddad says I'm twice as sweet. Granddad cries on the beach because I am never going to grow up, never going to be plucked from the tree by a handsome prince. My lovely granddad will never dance at my wedding because I now lie deep in the earth, among lichen-covered gravestones, next to a rugged elm. On my grave there are many sad wreaths, left by family and friends. The blooms, like me, are dead. Their petals wilt and the dog-eared cards of condolences warp and rot. "Dust to dust"; the wind will eventually blow them away.

In a lonely cemetery my body slowly decomposes.

Soon there will be very little left of me, only dried bones and decay. "Ashes to ashes", despite the fact my life has been snatched from me and my coffin is dark and cold, I'm pleased with my headstone. It is shiny new and made of polished granite. It has teddy bears adorning it. I love teddy bears, even when they are wet and weather-beaten. I wonder if other children will steal them or will they stay there long enough to rot away too?

I wanted to be a champion figure skater but now I won't be. You can't be a dancer when you are stiff and brittle like a broken twig. My skate boots are in the coffin with me, put there by my mother. A few days after my twelfth birthday I suddenly became famous, my name on the lips of everyone from my hometown. The local gazette even had my photograph on its front page.

The headline read, 'LOCAL GIRL BRUTALLY MURDERED'. A national paper carried the banner, 'GIRL'S BODY FOUND FLOATING IN RIVER'.

Fame came at a price; it broke the hearts of my family.

Because my family are sad, I am too.

Death steals everything but your memories. I remember my mother and my brother Jack, who is five years older than me. I love my mum more than anybody in the world, apart from my granddad, who always guesses what I'm thinking. Granddad makes me laugh and loves me a lot.

When I was alive, Jack hated me, he just did.

But now I'm dead he mourns me more than anybody.

When you love someone and they die, you are left only with the grief. When you waste your life disliking someone, death robs you of the opportunity to put things right. It leaves regret festering like a cancer in the heart. Remorse turns to guilt and shame burns the soul. Poor Jack is now filled with remorse.

Of course Jack didn't really hate me. He was just nasty, the way some boys and most brothers can be. He said he hated me, but that was because he didn't understand his moods. He *was confused; he'd never got over the fact our father had been killed. Daddy died thousands of miles away as I lay in Mummy's womb waiting to make my entrance into the world. I therefore never met him, and I think it's really sad that my father's lips never kissed me.*

Daddy was a soldier who lost his life in a war that started and ended whilst I was warm and snug in my mother's tummy. All deaths are a tragedy, but when you are blown to pieces before you ever hold the child you helped create, death must be extremely harsh.

To Jack, Daddy was a memory and a great loss. To me he was just a mirage, a military medal and a faded photograph; more a myth than flesh and bone. You can't miss something you never had. But when Daddy died, something in Jack died, too.

My brother was only five at the time but his pain was beyond bereavement. When the sweetest cream turns sour, there is no way to reverse it, nothing to look forward to but a fetid and bitter future. Jack's cream had turned and I was an intruder in a broken family. Like a confused cuckoo, I learned to survive in a hostile nest with an angry sibling.

Peace came to the South Atlantic but never crossed our doorway. That's the terrible thing about war; for some the pain continues long after the ceasefire.

Now I'm dead and Jack is bent over with guilt.

There is nothing I can do about it.

My best friend in the whole world is called Talia; everybody needs a friend to share secrets with. I told Talia things I would never tell anyone else, such as which boy I like the best. His name, by the way, is Adam. I have never kissed

Adam, but we both like Michael Jackson. I hoped someday to marry Adam, but I know now that is not going to happen.

My mum works for an estate agent, although she's on compassionate leave at the moment. She's a lovely mum; she taught me to dance and took me for my first ice-skating lesson. We had to take a ferry across the river and a bus ride to the rink, but on each part of the journey I got more excited.

I love skating.

On the ice I feel free, almost a grown-up.

When my granddad saw me skate for the first time, he clapped so loud, he nearly drowned out the music. Granddad is a Beach Boys fan, and because I love him so much, I often skate my routine to a Brian Wilson number.

I was a toddler when Torvill and Dean performed Ravel's Bolero and achieved a perfect score at the winter Olympics. I watched them on TV with my mummy. It's my earliest memory. Whenever I'm sad, I listen to the music and the Bolero takes me back to those warm and safe days. I dreamed of winning gold at a future Olympics, but I now know it's never going to happen.

Jack has no interest in ice skating; he thinks it's only for girls.

Two months before my last birthday, Jack bought REM's latest record, called MONSTER. When my broken body was pulled from the river, an angry Jack smashed the record and put it into the bin. I've never seen my brother cry before, but when you are tortured with remorse, perhaps the tears come easier. Jack put his monster into the trash, but walks in its shadow.

My monster is a killer of little girls. He is out there, a predator stalking. Like a big bad wolf, he's going to huff and blow, looking for his next little piggy, his next victim.

Chapter Three

The day Ellie was born, I rushed to the hospital. My daughter, Judy, was in the maternity unit while young Jack was being watched by some neighbours. I hurried from the car park and up the steps into the hospital. Frantically pushing past people in a crowded corridor, I passed a waiting room with a TV that showed the QE2 docking at Southampton returning our victorious troops back home. The whole country was in a jingoistic mood. Military bands played and the crowds on the quayside were ecstatic. Union Jack flags were flying and families were happy to be reunited. Tears of joy were everywhere.

I was anything but happy; perspiration beaded my forehead and I wore a shadow of grief across my eyes. My only child had just become both a new mother and a widow. Like collateral damage, the shrapnel from a grenade exploding thousands of miles away ravaged my daughter's family. The British army brought peace to the South Atlantic, but Judy's war would continue. No armistice or ceasefire for her, just the on-going battle to survive and a foxhole that was a cold lonely bed.

As my late wife would say, the triumphant song of life is not without its minor keys and discords.

I hurried past other new mothers in the ward and up to my daughter's bed. I noticed the empty cot. "Where's the baby?" I sounded anxious.

"It's all right, Dad. She's a little jaundiced. They're keeping her in an incubator in the side ward until her colour gets better." My daughter looked pale and she sounded tired, her hair a mess.

"When can I see her?"

"You can see her any time, just ask one of the nurses to show you. How's Jack?"

I shrugged and tried to sound upbeat. "He's fine. No problems. Have you decided on a name yet?"

"Yes, I'm going to call the baby Ellie, after Mum."

I smiled. "She would appreciate that. It's a pity she didn't live to see this day."

"Well, it seems baby Ellie will be having only one grandparent and one parent."

"Jack died fighting for something he believed in."

Judy started crying. "Doesn't help the pain, Dad, doesn't help at all."

"I'm sorry, pet. I don't know what to say except Jack would love the fact you have a daughter."

A long silence followed, a nurse passed the bed pushing a noisy tray on wheels with various medicines.

Judy wiped her tears with a tissue. "The army Chaplain came this morning. It seems we can't bring his body back. He'll be buried in the Falklands."

My eyes narrowed. "Bloody hell, that can't be right. They had no problem finding transport to get him down there. It's just not right. They should bring his body back. It's just not fair, just not fair." I said the next sentence to nobody in particular. The words just tumbled out. "The buggers buried my grandfather at the Somme in 1916, nothing's changed." Anger made my lips pinch into a thin line across my face. I eventually spat out, "They ask young men to fight and when they pay the ultimate price, it's as if the bloody government, once the war's over, just doesn't care."

"Go and see the baby, Dad. When you come back we'll talk about the future. We need to tell Jack, about his dad, he doesn't know yet. It'll break his young heart."

Minutes later I walked down a corridor and found the unit where the new baby was. I looked at my granddaughter and felt my heart melt. Wrapped up like a cocoon, she lay in an incubator asleep. I couldn't hide the proud look on my face as I whispered, "Hello Ellie, sweet pea, I'm your granddad." Her eyes opened, just for a few seconds. Her eyes were blue, although later they would darken to a pale chestnut colour. I know this sounds strange, but even then, a few hours old she seemed to possess a mesmeric power over me. Her striking eyes like a searchlight, blinded me in its beam. I swear I saw the whisper of a smile cover her lips.

Only when she knew I was under her spell did her eyes close and mine brimmed up.

A warm feeling of love flowed through my body. It was a magic moment and I knew my life would now be changed for ever. It would be dedicated to protecting this child, my lovely granddaughter, Ellie.

★★★★

Jack took the news of his father badly with tantrums and screams. The pain seemed to rip out his young heart. He smashed up his He-Men figurines. I didn't try to stop him. Better broken toy dolls than a broken five year-old boy. Judy came home and I decided to make a career decision. I needed to become a full-time granddad if Judy was to get her life in balance to save her sanity.

★★★★

"You want to do what?" My Chief Inspector's face went red as he nearly spilt his mug of tea.

I answered, "Early retirement I think it's called. I've got enough service in, checked it out with HR." My words seemed to drift over his head, so I added, "My daughter's husband has been killed in the Falklands and she needs help with the family. She's got a new born baby."

"Fucking hell, Tony. You've got at least another fourteen years left in you. There are plenty of people you can employ to do this sort of thing. I bet the army would help." He asked desperately, "Have you called the British Legion? There must be plenty of support out there." He put his mug down and pleaded. "I need you here. How about I give you some compassionate leave? You are, after all, my best detective."

I snapped back, "That's not what you said in my last appraisal."

His eyes narrowed and he spat out the words, "I knew you'd throw that up in my face. Fuck me, I told you, the Chief Constable was into fucking bell curves. I couldn't have too many fucking stars in the department. It was just your turn to take a knock." He gave a deep sigh, pausing to gather his thoughts. "Tell you what," he pointed an open hand towards me and sounding like a market stall holder said, "Stay and I'll promise you you'll get maximum ratings for the rest of your career." The anger drained from his face and a thin smile covered his lips. "How about that, it's a bloody good deal?"

I looked Chief Inspector Webster in the eye. I almost liked him; not a bad bloke, a bit thick but a good copper doing a difficult job. I replied, "It's a crock of shit. Besides, I need to go, my family need me." I said matter-of-fact, "There's bugger all you can do."

He looked angry again. "Fuck you. All the shit I wiped up after you. This is how you repay me?"

"I've paid my dues. My son-in-law has paid his, which means my daughter is now a war widow. I'll be leaving at the end of the month."

As my old boss's blood pressure went into orbit, I received a reduced pension. My wallet would be smaller. My car would have to rust and grow old with me and my dream of having enough money to last me a lifetime of holidays was swapped for a reality of having just enough money to last the month.

A small price, I thought, for protecting Ellie and helping her family.

I lived only two miles from their house, so most days I arrived early enough to let myself in and prepare breakfast before any one stirred from their bed. At first I stayed overnight, but I quickly learned that whilst the theory of natural selection hadn't yet abolished sleep, a young baby with good lungs, can. Ellie turned out to be a healthy child. She never suffered an illness that a spoonful of Calpol couldn't put right.

I tried to be a surrogate father to the two kids, but a granddad is just that; a granddad. However, I did learn some new things like how to change a nappy, something I hadn't done as a dad. I could also boil milk, change clothes, babysit and play in the garden with Jack.

He was a good lad and a talented footballer who wanted to become a professional. A few years later, I took him to Roker Park to watch the lads beat Bristol City. Jack's tall for his age, I'm nearly six feet in height and I think Jack takes after me. Ellie didn't seem to have any sporting aptitude and was only interested in playing with her dolls and teddy bears, but the day Judy took her the ice rink changed all that. Five years after that first visit and two weeks before her twelfth birthday, she entered into the North East Figure Skating Championship. I watched her with Judy and a rather sullen Jack as she skated to the music of the Beach Boys. The haunting melody of *God Only Knows* vibrated around the rink and the crowd held their breath. It was magical.

My granddaughter won the gold medal for the Under Twelves girls' section. I think she could have won Olympic gold with her performance. Ellie, with a triumphant smile, waved as the crowd stood on its feet and everyone clapped, with the exception of Jack, the stroppy teenager. Tears of high-octane pride welled up in me and I couldn't remember ever being so proud. Of course, the harrowing event awaiting us was only weeks away, something we didn't know that day. We only knew we were happy on home-brewed happiness. Funny how fragile happiness is and how easily nightmares can puncture your heart.

Chapter Four

*E*very summer the four of us went in Granddad's car to a caravan park in Keswick for our holidays. I loved the Lake District and Granddad would take us out in a rowing boat. As I got older we would walk up a local fell called Catbells and look at the magnificent panorama of Skiddaw and Derwent Water. The first time I walked up, Granddad had to coax me all the way up, but I made it. My family and I stood triumphant on the peak, and our reward was a boat ride back to Keswick for a fish and chip supper, paid for by Granddad. These were very happy days, but the happiest day of my life by far, was the day I won the gold medal.

I'd been skating for five years and found I could quickly master toe loops and counter turns, and within a year of starting I had my own coach, whose name was Jimmy. Jimmy's a bit fat and bald but he's clever on his feet. He used to be a boy champion, but I think that must have been around the time the dinosaurs roamed the earth. Granddad and Jimmy don't get on too well. I don't know why.

21

The night before the competition I couldn't sleep for excitement. I visualised each step in my dance routine and I imagined my Daddy was watching from heaven. I could hear his voice, "Come on Ellie." Of course I had no idea what his voice sounded like, but in my head he sounded like Tom Cruise.

I was listening to the birds welcoming another day, no, welcoming the BIG day, when I heard Granddad's key in the front door. I ran downstairs, jumping the last three steps.

"Hello, Granddad." I pushed open the kitchen door and saw him putting on the kettle.

"Hello sweetheart, you're up early."

I replied, "Couldn't sleep."

"Too excited, I guess. Never mind, I'm here to make your breakfast. Would you like an egg?"

"Please, please, please!" I clapped my hands.

"I'll make a fried egg on toast for your breakfast; food for a budding champion." He took the frying pan from the cupboard. "I bet young Jack's not up. He seems to be a champion sleeper. If there was a medal for sleeping in, Jack would win, no bother."

I joked, "We should change his name to Rip Van Winkle." As I sat down at the table I saw the kitchen door open and Mum walked in.

"Good morning, Dad." She turned and said to me, "You're up early, Ellie." My mum was already dressed.

I confessed, "Couldn't sleep, too excited."

"Well you need to go back up stairs and get dressed." Mum wagged her finger at me in a friendly manner. "You're not having breakfast in your nightie, even if today is a big day for you."

I pulled a face, but not being in the mood for an argument, I left the table and headed for the door.

Granddad called to me, "Remember young lady, you're never fully dressed until you put on a smile." I turned and grinned as he continued, "Did you know, to a man, the ultimate in feminine shapely curves is a good smile."

Laughing I replied, "Granddad, that's too much information."

Feeling more excited than I'd been for a long time, I scampered up the stairs two at a time. I heard Jack call out from behind his bedroom door, asking what the time was, but my mind was too full to bother answering him.

I was into my second egg, a reward from Granddad, when a glum Jack came down stairs. He wore the same expression and clothes he'd worn the day before and his hair needed combing. He walked towards the fridge, opened the door and lethargically took out a yogurt, tearing off its silver foil top. Picking up a teaspoon he started eating. I sometimes think my brother is a slob.

Mum said in a made-up cheerful voice, "Morning Jack."

Jack grunted before putting a spoonful of yogurt into his mouth. Jack's not very good with mornings.

"Ellie's had eggs, would you like some?" Granddad waited with a frying pan in his hand for a reply.

"No." Jack sniffed and turning to Mum pleaded, "Do I really have to go and watch Ellie ice skating?" He scratched his head, leaving some breakfast in his hair. "It's really boring."

Mum put on her not so made-up, angry voice. Raising her head and her voice she said, "We're a family Jack. You expect us to watch you at football. Now it's your sister's turn. It's not an option."

Jack muttered, "Brilliant." He looked at me, dagger eyes. "I hate ice skating, really, really hate it." With a sullen look on his face he threw the empty yogurt tub into the rubbish bin. He whispered to himself but loud enough for us all to hear. "It's just not fair. Hate it, hate it."

Granddad said softly, "Be careful, Jack. Hatred can be like an out-of-control missile that comes back and blows up in your face." Jack radiated fury and contempt as he stormed out the room and Granddad turned to me. "Don't worry about your brother, Ellie. Boys go through a lot of changes, makes them all moody. Jack doesn't mean what he says."

"I worry about the boy." Mum looked momentarily confused as she shook her head. She picked up my empty plate and walked away, placing it in the sink.

Granddad said reassuringly, "He's all right, Judy. Although I suspect he'll soon be graduating from yogurt to wild oats for breakfast."

Mum looking perturbed, stuttered, "Don't say that Dad."

I put on a puzzled face. "What do you mean, Granddad?"

Mum interrupted, "Too many questions young lady. Now get upstairs and gather your things."

"Yes," said Granddad. "We need to get there early for the best seats."

I giggled and held my hand to my mouth. "Granddad, what's the point of getting the best seats. You always stand when I'm performing."

"That's because I love watching you and I get really excited."

Upstairs we heard Jack slamming shut his bedroom door.

Granddad raised his eyes to the ceiling. "That lad is the only person I know who could slam shut a revolving door."

I thought, at least Adam is a nice boy. It was a pity he was in hospital and couldn't see me skate at the rink.

The four of us went in Granddad's car through the tunnel beneath the river. We continued towards the ice rink. Each mile increased my nerves so that by the time we arrived I felt quite faint. I picked up my bag from the back of the car and Granddad carried my skates.

"Do your best, Ellie." Granddad touched the top of my head. "Whatever happens will happen and we all love you."

Mum kissed my forehead and whispered reassuringly, "Best of luck, Ellie. We're all here and as Granddad said, do you best."

Granddad said, "You know who's going to win gold, don't you?"

"Who?" I had a puzzled look on my face. Granddad sounded as if he really knew.

He laughed and sang, "God Only Knows."

Mum laughed, "Granddad is being funny."

I half smiled, nerves holding back my sense of humour.

Jack said nothing as his smirk turned reptilian.

Taking the white bladed-shoes off Granddad, I left my family and walked towards the changing rooms. I was so tense, I forgot to wave goodbye.

Chapter Five

When I first met Jimmy Temple my old internal antenna pricked up, picking up his static. You can't make it in the police force, especially the detective squad, without good intuition. You quickly learn to recognise the criminal class just by looking at them. Can't explain, it's a perceptiveness; a trait all good coppers have.

Jimmy was Ellie's skating coach and when Ellie said I was a policeman, I saw the look. A certain shadow crossed his eyes. Of course Ellie forgot to mention I was retired, but I knew whilst Jimmy may not be a slime ball, he did have a past and it had nothing to do with ice skating.

A week later I sat in the County Hotel and opposite me sat DS Jill Adams. She used to be a DC in my team when I ran a detective squad. An ice maiden when at work, she had a large warm heart when off duty. We each had a beer on the table. She was a good detective, who kept no prisoners and could cut through bullshit like a laser beam. Her promotion was well deserved. Being a woman in a male-dominant police force made any career progress difficult, but she'd smashed the glass ceiling with her stiletto-heeled shoes and with a mixture of feminine charm and steely determination. She'd been into judo as a girl, and I'd seen her more than once throw some astonished thug to the floor with the ease Judy threw a pancake in the air.

I asked, "How's Webster?"

Jill shrugged. "Still angry with you." She looked thoughtful. "He seemed to be quite hurt when you retired."

"He thought I was owing to him," I said finally, clearing my throat.

Jill put her head to one side. "Are you?"

"I guess so."

"And?"

I paused and took a slug of beer. Returning the glass to the table I confessed in a whisper, "A few years ago, actually quite a few years ago, a suspect, a known drug dealer, suffered a broken arm whilst in my custody."

"And?" Her eyes narrowed.

"Webster helped cover it up. In the report we said the suspect had injured himself on the way to the cells, falling down the stairs."

Jill shook her head and said incredulously, "Tony, there are no stairs on the way to the cells, unless you were working out of the old Victorian police headquarters." She paused for effect then fired, "The one that was demolished in the 1950s!"

"I know!" I shrugged my shoulders before continuing, "Which is why Webster thought he'd done me a big favour. The druggie pulled something from his pocket and I honestly thought it was a knife. Turned out to be a smoking pipe he used for his habit. I used more force than could be considered reasonable. The Chief Constable at the time was very political and image conscious. The guy with the broken arm was mixed race. You can guess what the court and the papers would make of it."

She started, "Well, Webster's still angry …"

I raised my hand and she fell silent. "The good news was," I said brightly, "the drug dealer, once his arm was fixed, started going straight. He now lectures kids on the dangers of drugs; as they say 'always a silver lining'. Thanks to my intervention, I put a villain on the straight and narrow."

"Only now, you've got me off the straight and narrow, doing something I could get fired for."

"You're not the first copper to do something like this." I took another sip of beer and changing the subject, asked with a gentle voice, "How's that husband of yours, still at the bank?"

Her eyes narrowed. With her best police interrogating voice she said, "You've heard, haven't you?"

I admitted, "I heard a rumour."

She confessed as she gently rubbed the back of her neck. "It's true, we're separated." She said bitterly,

"Twenty years of marriage down the drain. I thought I married a banker, turned out he was a wanker; ran off with his secretary. He thought his pay and benefits included dipping his pen into the company ink."

I gave a sympathetic shrug. "Sorry about that, Jill. Being a copper is hard enough without all that crap."

"Thanks, Tony." She sounded sincere.

"It must be hard for you."

"You know me; I just get on with the job. Perhaps I didn't show him enough interest."

I tried to lighten up the mood. "Besides, I now suspect they'll be plenty of fresh pastures for you to explore."

She gave me an ironic look. "You're joking right? Plenty of fresh pastures, I'm getting too old to climb the fences."

I replied with a sensitive voice, "You too old?" I added, "I could show you how smart a detective I am by guessing your age," I paused and half smiled. "But it wouldn't be very bright, would it?"

She retorted, "Good decision, retired DI Bell, a very good decision. You should never guess a lady's age." She took a drink, placed the glass back on the table and gave me a coy look, which seemed to last for more seconds than it should have. She touched the side of my face and asked softly, "I guess you're not in any pasture, looking for a little TLC?"

I withdrew gracefully and with a wry look on my face, said, "What you're looking for is a father figure."

"You're not that old, Tony and you're still good looking. "She smiled and whispered in a conspiratorial tone, "No, what I'm looking for is what they call a sympathy shag. A good you know what without the usual hang ups."

I countered, "You don't beat about the bush, do you?"

Jill gave a schoolgirl giggle and raised an eyebrow. "Are you talking dirty, Tony?"

I grinned and shook my head at the same time. "Sorry, Jill, the only shags I know are the feathered ones sharing the cliffs with the gulls on Marsden Rock." I shrugged my shoulders. "It seems my field has a very high fence around it. Sad really, but it seems I was born to be a one woman man and she's dead."

She asked, "Don't you ever get lonely, Tony?"

I confessed, "Of course I do, who doesn't get lonely?"

"I mean really lonely, as if everybody else has stepped off the world and you're the last surviving human."

"All the time. You just have to bugger on, as Churchill would say and I bugger on in a corral without a gate."

"That's sad, Tony, real sad." She paused, "Anyway, I already knew your answer; it's just nice to pull your leg now you are no longer my boss. I hope you weren't offended."

I shrugged. "None taken." I took a breath and then asked, "So you weren't hitting on me, then?"

Jill came quickly back, "That's for me to know." She giggled then decided to come clean, "Actually I just wanted to shock you. I can't do that sort of thing back at the station; no more humour, we're always tip toeing around, careful with our language. I've had a stressful day and the force has changed a lot since you left, not all of it for the better."

As we let the silence stretch, I realised I was going a little rusty, no longer the sharpest Stanley knife in the police toolbox. In fact I was no longer in the box. The thought was neither disappointing nor otherwise; I was just who I was at that moment in time.

We were near a leaded window, and outside the glow from a lamp post illuminated the rain that was hammering down and a strong wind rattled the windowpanes. I like rain, because sometimes it washes away more than road dirt. When at home alone, I welcomed the rhythmic sound of water beating against the house and water rushing down the drainpipes. Best of all is the flash of lightning followed by the sound of thunder; it reminds me nature is far more powerful than any of us. At times like those, everything seems to take a pause and my lonely home becomes a refuge. I always pour myself a glass of whisky and enjoy the feeling of being secure in a dangerous world.

We sipped at our drinks for a moment before Jill changed the subject and asked, "So how's your daughter Judy and the kids?"

"All doing well. It would be a great help if Jack was like my new oven, self-cleaning." I paused for the joke to register, but when it only produced a half smile I continued, "And as you know, Ellie has starting ice skating."

"Hence this police report on a certain Jimmy Temple."

"You can't be too careful."

"You sound paranoid."

"The family has been through enough. What did you find?"

Jill swallowed hard. "I'm not a hundred per cent happy about this, Tony." A deep silence followed before she took out a folded A4 sheet of paper from her pocket. She surreptitiously handed it over and announced, "One speeding ticket and a few years ago, guess what?"

"What?"

"He got charged with GBH."

I clapped my hands in a triumphant gesture then tapped my nose three times. "I knew it; a good copper never loses his touch."

"Don't get too excited, Tony." Jill shook her head. "The case never came to court. Seems the victim was a retired priest and he dropped charges."

"What, he turned the other cheek?" I said sardonically, "How very Christian."

"Not really, it was pressure from his bishop. Seems our Jimmy was abused as a boy by said priest. Jimmy grew up and eventually got drunk one night. He came a-calling and gave the man of God a really good beating. I guess the priest probably deserved it."

I shook my head. "Bloody hell; no wonder the bishop wanted it all to be hush-hush."

It was Jill's turn to clap hands. It was obvious she was mocking me.

She pointed a finger at me and declared, "You *are* a good detective."

"Very funny, DS Adams." I paused before adding, "There is a problem, though."

"What's that?" Jill's eyes narrowed.

"People who are abused sometimes go on to be abusers themselves."

Jill threw me a cautious look and slowly shook her head. "You are paranoid."

"Paranoid enough to have words with Jimmy, and ensure little Ellie is always chaperoned when taking lessons. You've been a great help, Jill."

"Comes at a price I'm afraid." She drained her glass of beer."

"What do you mean, price?"

"If I can't have sex, I guess I'll have to screw you for a double whisky."

I looked at her. The reality was that even Sherlock Holmes couldn't have guessed her age; late forties, who knows? She was a good-looking blonde with few lines around the eyes, and the thought came to me that she was more Cagney than Lacey.

How had I not noticed before? The fact Jill looked a little like the actress, Sharon Gless, the smile was exactly the same, spontaneous and open. I felt stupid. All those years working together, I never noticed. Perhaps I'm not such a good detective after all, or maybe I'd been a little too focused on the job to notice a good-looking colleague. I stared too long and an exasperated look crossed her face.

She sighed and informed me, "It's a bribe, thank you."

I looked at her warmly. "No, thank you, Ms Adams," I stood up. "I'll get both of us a single malt."

Jimmy turned out to be a good coach. Ellie liked him and responded to his training methods. I mentioned the GBH to him and let it slide. He was resentful; perhaps the pain of his abuse was still raw. We acknowledged each other over the years, but never had another what you might call 'friendly conversation'. I told Judy about him and the need to ensure Ellie was always chaperoned. My daughter agreed with Jill; I was paranoid.

★★★★

Five years later and Ellie was in the North Eastern championships. I sat down on the wooden seats at the rink with Jack, who looked like a fella on his way to the gallows, and his anxious mother. Various competitions took place before it was Ellie's turn, and we sat and waited whilst the other competitors went through their routines. Ellie's section was strong and a few of the competitors scored highly. Silence came over the spectators as her name was announced. When Ellie glided onto the ice on her white skates, I could see she was nervous. The blood had drained from her face and my heart sank. I heard Judy take a short intake of breath. Ellie never looked so vulnerable. She was dressed in a new velvet dress, a turquoise number with blue glitter and shimmering sequins. She looked a picture, but I could see her confidence was as deflated as a punctured beach ball.

I muttered to myself, "Come on, sweet pea, you can do it." Judy stretched her hand out and grabbed mine. I heard her mumble something but it was too much of a murmur, I couldn't make out the words.

Ellie looked up and I think I caught her eye. She had the eyes of a frightened squirrel. I smiled and nodded. The music started; a track from the Beach Boys' Pet Sounds, *God Only Knows*. Ellie raised her head, bobbed a little curtsy and seemed to enter her own private zone.

She moved and with each glide of her blades her confidence grew. By the time she did her first turn her eyes had the steely look of determination and the whole audience knew it was watching something special. The marks for free skating are for technical merit, required elements and presentation.

I'm no expert and, hell, I was biased, but I knew Ellie was expressing true emotion and artistry that was beyond speech. To the sound of Brian Wilson's song, my mind took in the image of her moving in harmony with the music, a memory I will forever cherish like a valuable gem. To be an achiever you first must believe and Ellie looked like she believed she was the best ice skater at the rink, no, in the world. Her ambition to win the competition was tangible; her face radiated happiness and her toe loops were perfection.

The judges bent their heads and whispered to each other and then her scores were announced. The applause made the roof shudder, and as my granddaughter looked up at the standing ovation her face broke into the broadest smile I'd ever seen.

Moments like this only come a few times in one's life.

A tear emerged and before I could react and wipe it, it spilled quickly down my face and fell to the floor. Ellie won gold for her section and later that night, as I tucked her into bed, the medal was still around her neck. My heart was swollen with so much pride that the muscles on my face hurt with all the smiling.

Ellie, with her bed sheets pulled up to her chin, asked, "Was I good, Granddad?"

I was sitting on the bed, caressing her hair. "You mean when you were skating?"

"Yes."

Her eyes were like deep wells, hiding behind thick eyelashes. I smiled. "You won the gold, didn't you? So you must have been good."

"But how good? Was I really, really good, please tell me, Granddad?" My gorgeous Elle was searching for compliments. I thought, why not, if you can't fish for positive accolades when you're young, when can you?

I replied, "Well, let me tell you. Many years ago, before even MY granddad was born, there lived a group of painters and poets and they called themselves the Romantics. They looked for a spiritual dimension in their art that unites all things. They looked for spontaneous expression, believing all things shimmer with light and they only ever painted the most beautiful of women."

Ellie frowned. "What's that got to do with my skating?"

I replied with a gentle smile, "Well, they used a word when things went well, when it achieved that heightened interconnection between nature and art" I touched her nose. "Do you know what that word was?"

"No." Elle stared at me, as if her life depended on my answer.

I whispered, "The word was 'sublime'. It means something is inspiring, pure, perfection, even lofty and awesome."

Her eyes widened. "And?"

"You my darling, when you skated this afternoon were both sublime and supreme. You made me proud because you were perfect." I bent my head and kissed her forehead. "Goodnight, sweetheart, Granddad loves you very much."

"And I love you too."

My left cheek quivered and hell, another tear escaped and fell to the floor. Despite this, I left the room a very happy man.

Chapter Six

I was really, really scared. So scared I wanted to throw up. I'd changed into my new costume for the competition and Jimmy was giving me last minute instructions, but I couldn't hear what he was saying. Fear lubricated my tummy and I needed to go to the toilet twice. I was worried I might miss my slot and get disqualified. When it was time to leave the changing rooms Jimmy walked behind me, and maybe because I was going a bit too slow, he patted my bottom. A sort of 'hurry along' nudge. I spun around and said the words my Granddad had taught me to put off people I didn't like.

With a loud voice I said, "That was most inappropriate!"

Jimmy apologised immediately. "Sorry, Ellie, it was inappropriate. I'm just a little bit nervous."

Duh! Knowing he was nervous only made me MORE nervous.

When we got to the rink, a girl called Victoria was doing her routine. Her dad was a big solicitor in the area and she was a bit posh, although I still liked her.

Jimmy whispered in my ear. "Ellie, you need to forget everything."

Gasping and wide-eyed, I turned my head and asked, "What do you mean, Jimmy?"

"All the steps and your routine, if you think about it too much, you'll mess up."

I fought back the tears and my confusion and asked, "So how will I be able to do it?"

Jimmy replied with a soft voice. "You already know, your body knows too. You've practised this routine for months and worked hard. Believe me, just empty your mind, forget you are in a competition and you'll be fine." He added, "That's how I won my medal."

I heard my name over the PA system and my body seemed to leave me and float onto the ice. As if in a trance, I decided to follow. My little feet felt they didn't belong to me and my hands were clenched. I was alone and scared, surrounded by a sea of faces, all watching me. My little heart tapped away like hail on a tin roof.

A scene from a recent movie I'd seen about Christians and Romans flooded my brain. If fierce lions had emerged into the arena I wouldn't have been surprised.

I could feel the pulse throbbing in my temple; I looked up and saw Granddad, smiling at me, willing me to do my best. My heart slowed down a little and miraculously the tapping diminished.

A long pause. I took a deep breath as the musical introduction of God Only Knows started; synthesizer and French horns and I took another breath. It's a short introduction, but it was long enough for my stupor to fall away. As darkness lifts and rescues you from a nightmare, so the

39

music lifted my fears. My body seemed to whisper to me, "Don't worry, Ellie, we know what to do."

I was suddenly light and ecstatic at the same time. As if in a dream, I started my routine on the first word:

"I may not always love you
But long as there are stars above you
You never need to doubt it
I'll make you so sure about it
God only knows what I'd be without you."

I danced, twirled and glided over the ice. My complicated turns, arabesque spirals and axel jumps just happened. The only things I was aware of were the flash of cameras and my smile as it grew larger and larger. My feet and arms seemed to have a life of their own. It was as if angels were holding me up. It was impossible to fall down. I figure-skated a perfect dance.

When the Beach Boys and I finished, a roar of approval erupted around the gallery. I skimmed to the side where a smiling Jimmy held out his arms. He hugged my warm body and with an excited voice said, "Ellie, my little princess; that was flawless and pure textbook. I'm so proud of you." He kissed me on the cheek.

It was the first time Jimmy ever kissed me but I was too excited to care. I was on top of the world. Breathless from the skating, ecstasy sprang from my heart and I believed nothing could ruin this perfect day.

Waiting for the scores seemed to take ages; my fears slowly seeped back and my heart tapped again. The cathedral silence made my mouth go dry as my damp skin cooled down.

Eventually the judges announced their verdict and I screamed with joy.

I won Gold, GOLD!

I held my medal and my smile all the way home.

That night I lay in the bath and the thrill refused to diminish. Looking down I saw the wet ribbon and the medal resting on my tummy. I noticed my body was changing and I would probably surprise Mum next year by asking for a bra. I closed my eyes and imagined the scene and the words I would use to her.

I was starting to grow up in all sorts of ways. My thoughts drifted to the boy I loved and I dreamed of Adam sharing my bath water. The thought made me tingle all over as pleasure flowed through me like floodwater down a dry river bed. The unexpected sensuous goose bumps took me by surprise. I gripped the sides of the bath and tried to suppress a giggle.

Poor Adam was in hospital having his appendix removed. Talia made me laugh when she said he was having his penguin out. Even if Adam had been fit he wouldn't have come to see me skate, but I fooled myself that wasn't true. Then I had an idea; it was an awesome plan. When he's back home I'm going to go to his house and show him my medal. He's bound to be impressed. The thought made me happy.

Later when Granddad tucked me up in bed, he said I was a submarine. He's funny my granddad and he seemed to be very happy even though I noticed a tear run down his face.

My medal hung around my neck for days. At the recent Winter Olympics, Torvill and Dean had only won bronze medals. Submarine or not, I had done better than the best skaters in the country. Wicked! I was a golden girl, a golden submarine.

When I eventually took the medal off and put it on the side table next to my bed, it looked like a talisman, a lucky charm that would protect me from evil.

Well, that's what I believed then. Little did I know.

A few days later I bounced into Jack's room. I usually knocked, but I was still jaunty after winning the medal and just wasn't thinking straight. It was late afternoon and Jack was sitting on his bed with his back to the door. As I waltzed in his head spun around and his look stopped me dead.

"Get out!" He screamed, his face red and distorted.

I couldn't move. I wanted to explain why I hadn't knocked and what a silly sister he had, but his face turned dark with rage.

"Get out! Get out!"

I could see he was trying to hide something, but knew my curiosity would lead to a bitter argument and curiosity did kill the cat.

I turned and heard his voice, so full of anger. "Do that again and I'll kill you."

My brother is really a bad boy. He's so unfair. Just is. Are all brothers like this?

Chapter Seven

When I was a young constable, I got called to a domestic incident. A young boy, perhaps just in his teens, was smashing up his parent's house. The sight of my uniform did not pacify him and I watched in astonishment as he put a foot through the TV. I'd never seen so much anger in a young person, or was it frustration? He screamed like a banshee before exhaustion overcame him. I remember he answered my questions in a gawky, pedantic manner. He wasn't that many years younger than me, and when I tried a joke to calm things down I got the impression he didn't have a sense of humour. Social services got involved and it turned out he was suffering from Asperger's Syndrome, a psychological misfiring in his head. Social awkwardness and lack of empathy can be symptoms.

I sometimes look at our Jack and think he may have Asperger's, but then I think: Na, he's just a stroppy teenager; he'll grow out of it. Won't he?

Later, when I became a junior detective, I was part of a team investigating a missing person. We went to the house near the West Park, and because I was the youngest and therefore the fittest in the team, I was told to force my way in through an open window. The smell attacked my senses; a smell of death, so pungent, I couldn't extract it from my nostrils for days. The putrefied body of the missing person lay naked on top of a bed. He'd been dead for more than ten days. That's all the time it takes. Flesh decayed and maggots feasted on open pus wounds, while leaked excrement soiled the bed sheets.

The sight and stench haunted me. I've seen too many corpses over my career. Murder victims, suicides, road accidents, there is no good way to die. It was something I never got used to. Now I'm retired, I hope I never have to see another dead body, ever.

★★★★

"So what do you want for your birthday, Ellie?"

It was a week before her birthday and Ellie and I were walking through the sea-front funfair. We'd had just walked along the mile-long stone pier and watched some local men fishing. At the end of the pier, I'd showed her the secret miniature dolly in the wall of the lighthouse, put there by the Victorian workmen.

On our way back we saw a young seal basking on some steps near the water's edge. Ellie wondered if the parents had lost the seal and whether it was an orphan. We watched a large passenger boat sail through the harbour, heading up the river. Returning we'd strolled into the fairground with its flashing lights and I paid for a ticket so Ellie could ride on the carousel.

The fair was busy mostly with teenagers who walked around aimlessly, smoking, laughing and talking above the racket of loud pop music, which boomed out from the various rides. The smell of fish and chips hung in the air, while raucous gulls circled, looking for the opportunity to steal any dropped food.

My granddaughter was enjoying an icecream. I watched her with pleasure as she ran her tongue up the side of the cornet to capture some of the melting treat.

With a mischievous voice, she replied, "What would I like for my birthday? I would like my brother Jack to be nice to me, just for one day."

I joked back, "I'm your granddad. If you want miracles, you should ask God."

She gave me a puzzled look. "But why is Jack so horrid?"

I shook my head. "He's not horrid, sweetheart. It's just that he's going through that awkward stage in life, when everything seems *so unfair*." I imitated Jack's whinge on the last two words and Ellie nearly dropped her cornet, laughing.

She eventually asked, "Will I be horrid when I'm Jack's age?"

"No. Girls are made from sugar and spice; you'll remain just as nice when you are a teenager." I paused and put my arm around her shoulder and gave her a hug. "So, sweet pea, have you decided what you want for your birthday?"

She looked up at me. "I'd like to go to the cinema and see *Forrest Gump*; otherwise I'll just let you decide."

I already had. I'd bought her a wristwatch from Northern Goldsmiths, which had a colourful 'girlie' strap in red and yellow. The surprise present was wrapped up at my house, waiting for the birthday of its new owner. I informed her, "Okay, it's a date. I'll take you and the family to see Tom Hanks on your birthday this weekend."

"Thank you."

We walked from the fair to the sands, and as Ellie finished her icecream we sat down. More noisy seagulls circled overhead. They were apparently rowdy because we had the audacity to trespass onto their territory.

My young charge licked her fingers before wiping her hands on a handkerchief. She seemed distracted for a moment before saying, "Granddad."

"Yes, Ellie?"

"Can I ask you a question?"

"Of course, sweetheart."

She gave me a puzzled look. "How do you spell rhubarb?"

I had long got over my surprise at the range of questions my granddaughter would ask, so I closed one eye and answered slowly, "R-h-u-b-a-r-b."

Ellie thought for a moment then said. "That doesn't sound right. Why does rhubarb have an H?"

I rested my chin in my hands. "Ah, the byzantine puzzle they call English. It's the scourge of all foreign students. Sweetheart, the truth is many English words have silent letters; like 'debt', it has a silent 'B'."

"But why, Granddad?" Small furrows appeared on her forehead.

Hiding my mischievous tone as best as I could, I answered, "Well, let me tell you. A long time ago, the wise men who decided how to spell different words, decided 'rhubarb' had to have a silent 'H' in it to remind us what we need to put on our rhubarb."

The furrows deepened. "Do you mean custard? But that's a 'C'."

I laughed out loud. "No, I mean the 'H' is for Horse muck; the farmer has to put it on the rhubarb to make it grow."

Ellie's face twisted up in a comical mask. "Ugh, that's horrible." She demanded, "Are you telling me fibs again, Granddad?"

I shrugged my shoulders and put my head to one side. "Would I lie to you, sweetheart?"

Ellie said accusingly, "Jack says you do it all the time, something you learned when you were a policeman."

I said light-heartedly, "Jack should be arrested. He could then exercise his right to be silent. Also, a night

47

in the cells would make him appreciate his family more."

Ellie grinned at the thought. "What about that other word?"

"What other word?"

"The word you mentioned, before."

"You mean 'debt'?"

"Yes, why does it have a silent 'B'?"

I smiled and suppressed a grin. "Debt has a silent 'B' to remind you some **b**ugger owes you money."

"Granddad!"

Laughing out loud, we both fell onto our backs on the sand, holding our bellies.

We laughed so loud, we frightened off the gulls.

★★★★

I once attended a police conference called Anarchy and the Breakdown of Civil Society. It was early in my career and the main thrust of the talk was society is very fragile and civil unrest simmers just under the surface. The speaker suggested that if you removed just seven meals from the population, you'd end up with a hungry rabble on your hands and all acceptable lawful behaviour would break down. 'Just seven meals' was his mantra which he kept repeating.

Call me a cynic, but I thought he was being optimistic. I had a dog at the time, a domesticated animal. It had taken thousands of years of breeding to produce this docile creature. But I knew the dog, even as it licked my hand, was just two meals away from being a wolf.

Breeding among people is more haphazard. There's no kennel club to watch our pedigree. The result is we all have the barbarian primate dwelling inside; it's just in some people the beast is too near the surface. As a detective I've trawled the cesspool of humanity doing my job and, believe me, feral families exist. Their bellies are full of junk food, but they are starved of ambition and good manners. Fast food and slow minds. They didn't need the excuse of missing meals to behave in an abhorrent manner. Theirs was an underworld where druggies howl at the moon, while knife-carrying savages dress in blue jeans and louts wear designer trainers. Criminal behaviour was the norm. 'Thugs are us'!

My police service investigation sheet covered every crime against common decency from incest to multiple murders. That's why I'm so protective of my family, and why I had to retire early to look after them. My daughter thinks I'm paranoid, but I've looked into the face of humanity and believe me, it's ugly.

Ellie came into the kitchen. Judy had already left for work and young Jack hadn't left the messy cave he called a bedroom. Brian Matthews was talking on the radio.

I said, "Morning, Ellie, are you still a vegetarian?"

"No, Granddad, please keep up, that was last week." She pulled out a chair from the table and sat down.

"So you can have a bacon sarnie for breakfast?"

"Guess so. Please put lots of tomato ketchup on though. I still love my vegetables."

"I think tomatoes are a fruit. Do you want your bread toasted?"

"Toasted please. Today is Saturday, right?"

"Yes, young lady, *Sounds of the Sixties* is on the radio and that tells you it's a Saturday." I dropped two rashers into the frying pan.

"Whatever. Granddad can I ask you a question?"

"You can, but 'MAY I ask you a question' is better."

"Whatever." She scratched the back of her head. "Did you know my daddy?"

I turned from the frying bacon and replied, "Of course I knew him."

She leaned back on the chair, balancing on the back legs. "Please tell me what he was like?"

"Why do you want to know?"

"I just do, please."

I paused as I gathered my thoughts. Smiling I replied, "Your daddy married my daughter, your mum, and I was very happy. I wouldn't have been happy if I hadn't liked him. I enjoyed having a pint with him. He was very intelligent and loved his job. I remember he was a good darts player."

"Cool. Did he have any other girlfriends before meeting Mummy?"

I looked at her with surprise. "That's a strange question, why do you ask?"

She shrugged. "I'm just wondering." She sat forward, putting the chair's four legs back on the floor.

"I guess he may have, but it was your mum he loved and from that love you and Jack were born."

Ellie hesitated then said, "I wish Daddy hadn't been killed."

I replied dolefully, "We all do, sweetheart. But your daddy was a soldier and sometimes soldiers get killed. My granddaddy was killed in war. It's a cruel world; people do die."

"But Mum is so sad; I think she still misses Daddy."

"Of course she misses your daddy, but he wouldn't want us to be sad, he would want us to be happy and remember him with fond memories."

Ellie's mouth turned downwards like a horseshoe and she made a helpless gesture. "But I can't remember him."

"Well, that's because he died before you were born, sweetheart, but I'm sure your daddy looks down and is really proud of his daughter."

Ellie's face brightened up. "Do you think so, Granddad?"

I put her breakfast down in front of her. "I'm positive, Ellie, it wouldn't make sense if it didn't happen. Now have your breakfast. I can hear Jack upstairs, he's up; have your bacon in peace whilst you can."

"Do you think he watches when I ice skate? I hope he does."

"I'm sure he does."

"I love you Granddad."

"I love you, sweetheart." I bent and kissed the top of her head.

I was pleased with myself because I had told the truth, but somehow I also felt guilty, as if I'd lied to every question. I really did like Jack senior. The shock of his death was as devastating to me as it was to the others; he was a well-loved son-in-law and I missed him, too.

Chapter Eight

*A*wesome, it's only five days before my birthday. I was with
my best friend, Talia, in her bedroom. Around Talia's
room, just like mine, her much-loved, childish cuddly toys
looked up at grown-up pop posters. Of course, my bedroom,
like all girls' bedrooms, is the place where I dream of boys and
wild, improbable romance, whilst hugging a soft teddy bear.

School was finished for the day. Talia and I sat in front of
the mirror brushing our hair, laughing about nothing. Funny
when you're young how you can giggle for ages with a best
friend over nothing. It has to be a best friend, though; you can't
laugh at nothing with someone you don't like. It's not how it
works.

Talia had brought me over to show off the new leather
shoes her mother had bought her. Afterwards she started
rattling off various lists of unfair teachers, nice teachers, girls
who were her friend, girls she'd fallen out with, girls who wore
their skirts too short, girls who wore their skirts too long, who
had the nicest colour hair, which boys she liked, boys she didn't

like. Talia seemed to carry umpteen lists in her head. I smiled through each listing and for the sake of our friendship, agreed with each one.

A record was playing Love is all Around *by Wet, Wet, Wet. Talia had a poster of Kurt Cobain on the wall. I had a similar picture in my bedroom with another poster of Bon Jovi. He looked down into my refuge from a scary world.*

Talia inquired, "Why do you have red hair, Ellie?"

I replied hastily, "Granddad said I have red hair because my ancestors were Vikings. I come from a fierce band of Norsemen."

"Do you like having red hair?"

"I love it." It was an honest answer.

"When I'm older, I'm going to dye my hair blonde, like Madonna."

The room fell quiet, so I said, "By the time you're old enough to dye your hair Madonna will be an old lady."

Talia giggled then announced to my reflection, "Guess what I saw today? I saw Mr Haines holding hands with Miss Hawley."

"No!" I expressed shock and stopped brushing. The couple mentioned were teachers on Talia's 'likeable' list. "Were they kissing?"

"No, silly, I told you." Talia put her brush down and looked at me, "They were just holding hands. They looked so cute."

My eyes narrowed. "I don't believe you."

She turned her head back to the mirror and said, "I don't care. I know what I saw. They were holding hands and talking. Miss Hawley was also smoking a cigarette. She told us she didn't smoke, why do adults lie so much?"

"Where did you see them?"

She announced gleefully, "In the car park. They sneaked into Mr Haines' car."

"Did they see you?"

"Don't think so, I was hiding behind a bush."

"Awesome."

She turned her face towards mine. "Do you think they love each other?"

I raised my eyebrows, "Must do if they're holding hands, people don't hold hands unless they're in love."

She gave me a quizzical look. "You love Adam, but you haven't held his hand, yet?"

I answered quickly, "But I will do one day. I'll kiss him too."

Talia was thoughtful. "Do you remember when Miss Hawley told us about boys injecting?"

I paused before replying, "You are such a silly girl, I think you mean, 'ejaculation'."

"I'm not silly, you are."

"Whatever."

"Whatever, anyway do you know boys do it when they dream?"

I retorted, "Miss Hawley said it was called a wet dream."

Talia giggled for ages and I caught the bug and giggled with her.

Eventually I stated, "Miss Hawley said," I put on a posh voice, mimicking our sex education teacher, "it is perfectly normal and natural for boys to have a wet dream. Boys shouldn't be afraid when it happens."

Talia was holding her tummy, struggling to catch her breath as she laughed.

I continued, "Remember when she showed us the condom and demonstrated with a banana?"

Talia couldn't speak and only managed to nod.

I said conspiratorially, "Well last year a boy and a girl went behind the school sheds after the condom lesson. The boy asked for sex and the girl agreed, but only if he used a condom. So they had sex and the girl felt something warm inside her and asked him if he was using a condom. 'Yes,' said the boy and he showed her his banana with the rubber on."

Talia fell off her stool laughing at the joke and the two of us were hysterical for absolutely ages.

Eventually, Talia rubbed her eyes and mumbled, "That was really wicked, Ellie." She looked at me gooey-eyed, "I wonder what it will feel like to kiss a boy? I bet it's really wicked."

I nudged her with my elbow and replied enthusiastically, "You can do this, to get an idea." I kissed the fleshy part of my arm.

Talia copied me and started kissing her arm, making all sorts of silly noises. I burst out laughing.

Talia said, "Do you want to try it with lipstick?" Before I could answer, she rushed out of the room and came back with her mother's red lipstick. She sat in front of the mirror and applied some to her lips. It looked like Talia had done this before. I quickly followed, putting some onto my lips. We started kissing our forearms passionately making all sorts of silly girlie giggles. Our arms were smudged in bright red kisses. Suddenly, without an explanation, an excited Talia ran from the room and came back carrying a bottle of her mother's perfume. She sat down breathless and squirted a cloud over herself before spaying a fine mist over my head.

"There," she said, "that's really fab. We smell as well as look grown-up." We applied more lipstick and giggled until our faces hurt. Talia asked with a serious voice, "Do you want to kiss my lips, to see how it feels?"

Before I could answer, she leaned over and our red lips met. The record stopped playing its music and Talia's eyes sparkled. "That was nice. Do you know some women only like kissing other women?"

I asked hesitantly, "Why?"

"I don't know. They must just like it."

"I think when I kiss Adam it's going to be fabulous. He's so cute, I just can't wait."

Talia confessed with a giggle, "I can't wait either. I have to go for a pee."

With that my sniggering friend left the room, shutting the door with a clash. I heard her as she ran along the landing to the bathroom. I turned my head towards the mirror, with its fluffy pink ribbons surrounding it. I realised I really wanted to kiss ADAM. I'd had the urge before, but now it seemed to overwhelm me, like the waves on the beach. When the sea wave swept me off my feet I would feel frightened. Now this other wave made me warm all over. Adam was the best looking boy in the school, no in the whole world! Why would I not want to kiss him?

I brought my lips to the fleshy part of my right arm and sucked hard. I'd seen older girls with love bites on their necks, a badge of honour for making it to 'first base', whatever that is. I wanted that badge, even if it was only on my arm and DIY. Why had God made us so it was impossible to kiss one's own neck?

I didn't hear the bedroom door open.

"What are you doing?" It was a man's voice.

I spun around and there in the doorway, stood a man, I recognised him as Talia's uncle.

I felt my face blush up as I brought my arm down from my lips.

Her uncle queried, "Where's Talia?"

The man looked middle-aged. He didn't sound angry, but he didn't sound friendly either.

I stuttered, "She's gone to the bathroom." I felt a cold shiver go down my spine, my warm wave washed away leaving a tidemark of some emotion I didn't understand, but I instinctually knew it was to do with the way this man was looking at me. I looked at him, opened mouthed.

He demanded, "What have you got on your lips?"

I didn't answer. I felt frozen to the seat. Cornered like a trapped animal, I turned my face away from my interrogator, hoping the feeling of guilt would subside. I could see his reflection in the mirror.

I heard him say, "You do know naughty girls get smacked bottoms."

My hand slowly came up to my mouth, to wipe and remove the stolen lipstick.

He almost pleaded, "Why no, don't do that, pet." Smiling, but without any warmth he walked up behind my chair. I could see his mirror image as he breathed in the perfume. His eyes looked glazed, dead like the eyes of my dolls. He touched my locks, very gently, almost a caress. His eyes closed for a second and then he looked into my mirrored eyes that stared unblinking. He whispered, "Your hair is wonderful and the lipstick suits you. You look quite grown-up. Why man, you look almost like a woman, not a silly school girl anymore." He paused, staring with a look I didn't understand. He sighed and whatever had been going on in his head vanished. He said sharply, "Do me a favour, pet. Tell Talia when she returns, her mum says tea is ready." He turned and left the room, but my cold feeling remained.

Later, as I said goodbye to Talia at her door, our faces were refreshed and we had no traces of lipstick on our lips. I turned and as I ran all the way home, I could hear a man's laughter echoing in my head, like the howl of a wolf.

Next day Granddad took Jack fishing. They went off together once a month. Granddad calls it 'bonding' and says it's a man thing. When they came back, Jack was really angry. They had travelled up the river and been fly-fishing. Apparently, it requires more skill than when you fish from the sea, but I don't understand the difference. Granddad said Jack was so good at casting he could land a fly on a five pence piece from fifty yards. I think it's a silly way to spend an afternoon, but then I'm not a boy.

Jack angrily threw his bags on the kitchen floor. Mum and I were sitting at the table; something nice was baking in the oven.

Jack snarled, "Bloody hell, I lost my landing net." He looked like he was ready to cry.

Mum looked up in concern.

"Don't swear, son." Granddad placed his bags carefully on the floor and leaned his rod against the wall. "We can always get another."

Jack continued angrily. "I would have landed that salmon, if the bloody net hadn't slipped out of my hand. It was huge, probably the best size fish I've EVER caught."

"Oh dear," said Mum. "Never mind, we can always get another one."

Irritation and frustration made Jack spit out, "You just don't understand, the net belonged to Dad, I've lost it, it's probably out to sea now, heading for Norway."

"It's only a net, Jack." I tried to pacify him. "What was SO important about a silly net?"

Jack jerked his head towards me and screamed, "You are such a stupid girl, why can't you think before you open that mouth of yours. Why have I got to have such a dense sister?" He breathed in, inflating his chest as if loading a gun then fired both barrels. "I wish you had never been born."

"Jack!" Mother got up from the table as much shocked as angry.

Jack continued his tirade. "It's like my whole life is messed up. It's just so unfair. I get the biggest fish and lose both my dad's net and the salmon. It's just a bloody mess. I hate this family!"

Granddad took off his hat and kept quiet. He'd told me many times, sometimes it's best to let a storm come to a natural end and not to fight nature.

Mum of course didn't understand nature or storms. She said, "Jack, I know you are angry, but it will pass, it's not that important. But you need to apologise to your sister. What you said was cruel."

I knew Jack wouldn't say sorry and the family fight would get worse. I hated fights, I just didn't understand them; in the same way I didn't understand fishing. So I added, "Yes, Jack, losing the net is not important."

Jack screamed and pointed at me, "I'll tell you how important it is! I wish it was you floating down the river not my dad's net."

Mum's voice filled the room. "That's enough, Jack, go to your room and don't come down until you're in a better mood." She sounded at the end of her tether.

As he walked away, Jack turned at the door and looked straight at me. Anger was still in his eyes. He mouthed something so the two others couldn't hear. But I watched his lips and read his message: *I WISH YOU WERE DEAD.*

Why are brothers so nasty, especially mine?

Granddad smiled and looked a little bit embarrassed. He had taught me that nature hates a vacuum, so I created a happy thought for myself: it was only a few days to my birthday.

The next night Mum had a date. She always insists it really isn't a date, just a dinner with her boss from work. His name is Harry and he has never been married. He was the same age as Mum, but Jack thought him a loser because he supported Newcastle United. It seemed our town was equal distance from Newcastle United and Sunderland, which meant the town was split between the two lots of supporters. Two tribes loving football but hating each other; then again when one team's nickname is the Magpies and the other is the Black Cats, is it any wonder they fight?. Like fishing, it was all beyond me.

Mum's boss likes curry, really hot and spicy. Mum hates Indian food but hasn't told him yet. Harry also plays squash but that hasn't stopped the emerging beer belly. Because of his pot belly and the smell of curry, I can't imagine Mum ever *wanting to kiss Harry, so it's okay they dine together. I imagine they talk about office things. I like Harry because Jack hates him as much as he hates me. I think Jack hates Harry because he's a little bit jealous. Granddad says nothing, just comes around to babysit the two of us. We are allowed to watch anything on telly as long as Granddad is interested. For example, Granddad will watch any re-runs of* Top of The Pops *circa 1960's, but we never see a current one, although we all like* Animal Hospital *and* Mr Bean. *Even Jack laughs at* Mr Bean. *Granddad's favourite TV show by far is* Crime Watch, *but when it's on Jack and I go to our bedrooms to do our own thing.*

Later that night I was in bed, nearly asleep, when I heard Mum and Harry returning to the house. They were arguing next to the front gate. I could hear Harry's voice. He was ever so loud, too much beer I thought, but I heard an angry Mum send him on his way with a flea in his ear. I hoped Mum and Harry would be on more friendly terms next day at the office.

When Mum came in the front door, I heard an anxious Jack shout from his bedroom, "Are you all right, Mum?"

Granddad's voice came up the stairs. "It's all right, Jack. Mum's back home now, we'll look after her, won't we lad?" There was a pause and Granddad said, "Get to sleep, Jack. See you in the morning."

Jack grunted and I could hear muffled voices coming from down stairs.

I hoped they were discussing my birthday, only a few days away. A few minutes later, the hypnotic sound of rain against the window lulled me into a deep sleep.

Chapter Nine

Years ago my wife sent me a wedding anniversary card. She penned in it:

"There is only one happiness in life, to LOVE and be loved."

It was a quote from George Sand, the French writer. When my wife wrote it, she knew she was dying. The illness took her away six months later. I still have the card and often look at it. It gives me comfort because I miss her so much. I believe love is endless joy and endlessly interesting. Okay, I know love can destroy but it is also salvation. I experienced true love and I don't think I can ever love again with such desire. Sometimes when I lie in bed, in the early hours of the morning, when loneliness is my only companion, I feel my wife's presence, but I know it's only the cold feeling of isolation driving my imagination into overdrive.

Of course there's the other love: love for the family and my love for them consumes me, but I wouldn't want it any other way.

I was a hard-boiled copper, so I know the score. This is your life, pal. It's not a dress rehearsal, no second chances. As I've told many a sorry-looking villain as I cuffed them, "don't do the crime if you can't do the time."

My wife and I only had the one child, Judy. I worked hard, lots of unsociable hours. Fighting crime is not a nine-to-five job, it's a twenty-four-seven vocation, with most crooks working the night shift. I was home very little in the early days, missing most school sports days. Her mum died when Judy was fifteen years of age. Life can suck; teenage years are hard enough without losing your mum. I'm not sure how good a father I was. Okay, I probably do and I'm not proud of my record, but I'm determined to be the best granddad I can be.

I owe it to my late wife.

★★★★

Jack senior, apart from being a good soldier and husband, had been a keen fisherman. Because of this, I felt obliged to teach his son, young Jack, how to fish, although at the beginning, I had no enthusiasm for the sport. We started fishing off the big pier, kitted out with lugworm and large brass reels, but we slowly graduated to the more subtle art of fly-fishing. The river had been cleaned up as the industrial landscape changed. This had been bad news for all the shipyard workers, welders and shipwrights, but great news for the salmon that returned to a cleaner river after an absence of hundreds of years.

Fishing helps to calm Jack down and he seemed to have a natural talent for casting, while I found a hidden flair for making artificial flies. Jack soon learned that by using his wrist and forearm, and looping the line over his head, he could spot-target the almost weightless fly. It's a very complicated skill, and Jack, I believe, didn't realise how hard it was, so with youthful naivety he was soon able to land with precision a fly onto a coin from fifty yards away. He was a natural and even I was impressed.

Armed with our licenses and equipment, we became a bit of a star team on a stretch of the river near Hexham, about thirty miles from the mouth of the river. A few days before Ellie's birthday, I took Jack in my car to our favourite place, a bend in the river a few miles upstream to the bridge at Hexham. The water stretched between two banks about fifty yards apart, and was both shallow and deep in parts, with some benign eddies and others that were dangerous. I was strong enough in the arms to skim a stone to the far bank.

I was hoping for a peaceful day and it should have been, with a beautiful blue, September sky and the salmon running. A great opportunity, I thought, for a bit of bonding with my grandson. I should have known. How one's expectations so easily get screwed up.

Jack inherited his father's fishing equipment: an eight-foot rod with full flex and a vintage reel. To a grieving boy they were like religious relics, a tangible link to happier times. Jack protected them with the same zeal as a Knights Templar guarding the Holy Grail. I was not even allowed to touch the rod.

It took an hour drive to reach our favourite fishing spot and Jack remained silent through most of the journey. He pulled on his waders, and standing in the water he started casting. I stood on the bank a few yards away using my own rod and a technique called 'reach casting', which enables the line to drop on the water in such a way so as to produce less drag.

After twenty minutes, Jack turned and speaking loudly so I could hear, asked, "Do you think they'll bite today?"

"I hope so; otherwise I've wasted a load of petrol."

"I'm feeling lucky."

I paused and in between casting asked, "What are you going to buy Ellie for her birthday?"

A further pause ensued with only the sound of running water as the river rippled past us.

Eventually I asked, "You are going to get her something, aren't you?"

Jack remained silent. Finally he nodded a few times, very slowly. "Of course," he murmured. "I'll buy her something."

I fell into a long silence, searching for the words that would not upset my grandson. The policeman in me wouldn't let the question go away, although I knew it would be futile. Perhaps I lived in hope. "Why don't you get on with your sister?" I felt my hands go numb as I played with my line, making me wish I'd pulled on my gloves. Autumn was already in the air. The leaves on the trees on the far bank were turning russet, nature's notice that summer was on its way out.

Jack didn't react to my question, possibly because he didn't know the answer. I suppose a psychologist would say he resented her replacing his dead father; or that every time he saw Ellie it reminded him, deep in his mind, of the pain of losing a dad. Anyway, the resentment was subterranean and, although he never used violence against his sister, I always got the impression it was just below the surface, festering away like a tumour. I was not angry with Jack, just disappointed that I seemed to have failed as the granddad. How do you banish the bitter memories from a young mind? What fiction went on in his young head? What biography did he pen in his imagination? What was it that Jack wanted?

I spent many a night thinking about the puzzle that was Jack, pondering what advice I could give and what rational arguments I could use. But I was a copper, used to facts not emotions, and in Jack's universe there were too many things that escaped my understanding. The truth was: Jack was a stranger to his own family.

A few hours later, after we'd eaten some food, Jack was back in the water. Neither of us had caught anything and I could hear a song bird in the trees. Jack was casting into deep water under the shadow of a big willow tree, and I seriously thought about calling it a day when he shouted.

"I've got one, it's big!"

I put my rod on the ground and ran the few yards to Jack. His rod was bent and straining to breaking point; it was a big one.

I shouted, "Keep playing it, son. It's a whopper, best catch to date I would say." I was breathless with excitement. What is it that makes males get so animated in catching food? Is it the primeval instinct of the hunter gatherer? Who knows? All I can say is I was shouting and whooping like a teenager, losing my footing and sliding on the greasy bank where I landed heavily on my backside. Jack laughed as he expertly started to draw in his catch. The large tail splashed out of the water two or three times and I held my breath.

Jack turned and looked at me. "Don't just sit there. Go and get my net." He turned his eyes back towards his prey, the salmon that pulled on the line in a fight for its life.

I ran towards the car and looked in the trunk. The landing net was there and I took it out and extended the rod-handle. Like all Jack's equipment, the net had belonged to his dad. I ran back to the riverbank, now sweating and breathless. Jack had to move a few feet towards me as I stretched out the handle of the net. Net in hand, he started to pull and spin his line, bringing the fighting fish closer to him. I wished I'd been wearing waders, so I could go into the cold water and help.

The fish was almost in the net when it happened.

The first indication was the distant barking of a dog. The barking got louder and three animals crashed through the undergrowth and into the river. With panic-stricken eyes and white froth bubbling at their mouths, the spooked cows charged into the water only a few yards from Jack. The dog had scared them and now they were out of control like a trio of runaway trucks, bearing down on him. The avalanche of bovine assassins made the most appalling bellowing sound, as they thundered and threatened to run over my grandson.

I froze, shocked into inaction. Jack, his face distorted with fear and shock, fell with a splash into the water as the animals ran past. In the confusion, he let go of his landing net.

When your waders are filled with water, there is a real threat of being dragged down to the bottom and drowning, but Jack had been well trained. Lying on his back, his head above water he reached out to the bank with his rod. I grabbed it and hauled him to the bankside. There was no need for a landing net to bring him ashore. On all fours he slowly dragged himself, like a half drowned badger, onto the grassy bank and fell on his back, his eyes closed. The salmon was gone and I looked for the net but it was also gone, captured by the current and heading down stream.

I took a sodden Jack to Hexham, found a laundrette and washed and dried his clothes whilst he, trembling with cold, sat in the car, feeling sorry for himself. My grandson sat in the back of the car for the journey home and I heard him burst into tears, sobbing like I'd never seen him before. I looked into the mirror to catch his eyes, but despair bent his head and I only saw the top of his head.

★★★★

Harry, Judy's boss, wasn't what you'd call an alpha male. Occasionally, he'd call and they'd go out for dinner. He wasn't her sort. Her husband, Jack, had been her type of bloke; Harry was more 'harried' than a 'Jack the lad', if you get my drift.

The truth was, I'd more chance of finding Lord Lucan than Harry had of romancing my daughter.

Even though the relationship was platonic, young Jack was jealous and didn't mind letting his feelings be known. The night after the cows in the river incident, I babysat the two grandchildren whilst Harry took Judy out for a meal.

He would always tell me they would be discussing office business, as if he needed an alibi.

The kids were getting too old for a babysitter, but it was a ritual as inflexible as granite, that none of us wanted to end. It was *Crime Watch* night, so I knew I'd have no difficulty getting the two to go to their rooms and to bed. We had the usual fight about me wanting them to sleep with an open window.

It was about 11pm when I heard voices outside the front door.

I opened the door and saw Judy down the path, arguing with Harry. He was holding up his right arm, as if trying to protect himself.

The light from the hallway illuminated the garden and Judy turned and marched towards the door. I stepped inside and she slammed the door and leaned against it. I could see she'd been crying. Jack shouted down if everything was all right. I told him everything was okay and to go back to sleep.

In the kitchen I put the kettle on. I asked in a fatherly way, "Want to talk about it?"

Judy shook her head and dabbed her eyes with a tissue.

As I made the tea she said, "It's bloody Harry. Made a clumsy pass at me, I slapped him. Now I'll have to leave my job and I need the money." She opened her mouth to say something else, but the words stuck in her throat.

I poured two cups of Earl Grey and said, "You don't have to leave; you've done nothing wrong." I handed her a cup.

"How can I work in the same office? It'll be hell. Besides, he could make my life very awkward."

"Who's Harry's boss?"

"Some regional manager, don't know his name."

"Well, let me tell you something, my girl. Harry is going to wake up in the morning sober and he's going to feel very afraid. You could sue both him and the company for harassment. They would sack him in the blink of an eye. I'll have words with him in the morning."

Judy shot out her arm and touched my shoulder. There was fear in her eyes. "No Dad, it'll only make it worse."

I shrugged. "How?"

She had a haunted look. "My dad going to see the boss, it'll be like I'm a school girl and you're going to see the headmaster. What do you think the rest of the staff will think with you shouting in the office?"

I took hold of her hand. "I promise I won't shout."

Judy murmured, "You've broken that promise before."

"When?" I sat back in my chair.

"When I told you I was pregnant with young Jack." Judy smiled bitterly.

"Oh, then!" I put my head to one side and said very softly, "Well you were very young and not exactly married were you?"

"I was by the time Jack came along. Happily married too, in fact, I was too bloody happy. Now it seems I can't move on."

"Are you good at your job?"

"Of course I am and before you ask, I'm very happy with it. I'm a good estate agent."

I took a deep breath and took a drink of my tea. As I put the cup down, I spoke slowly. "I'll have words with an ex- colleague, Ms Adams. She'll talk to Harry, in a discreet way, on the phone. Believe me the threat of police procedures will take any smile off his face. It's going to be okay." I felt muscle twitch on my face and guessed it must have looked like a conspiratorial smile.

"Are you sure, Dad?"

"That's what dads do, look after their family. I promise nothing is going to happen to you or the children. There's nothing more powerful than a promise and this promise won't get broken."

After kissing my daughter goodnight, I walked back home in rain that fell like a curtain of tears, a forecast of things to come. I thought at least young Jack is going to be happy. No more Harry and his mum smelling of curry. I didn't know it then, but in a few days my promise would be broken, smashed into a thousand pieces.

Chapter Ten

I was filled with joy. How happy could one girl be?

That day was my birthday and how exciting was that? I was going to get presents from Mum, Jack and a Swatch watch from Granddad. (I managed to squeeze the truth from him. He said with my interrogation skills I should consider getting a job with the CID). Also we were all going that night to see Tom Hanks in Forrest Gump. But the most awesome present of all was that Adam was out of hospital, and I was going to go to his house to show him my medal. I was convinced he would be so impressed. Adam might kiss me, especially when I told him it was my birthday!

Medal + birthday = KISS

Wicked!

I dreamed he'd kiss me the way Tom Cruise kissed Kelly what's- her-name in Top Gun: Adam, PLEASE TAKE MY BREATH AWAY.

I just know he will.

Mum gave me a Nadia CD (loved it) and a coat. It's lovely, makes me feel grown up. I'm going to wear it when I go to Adam's. Jack gave me a card and a large bar of chocolate, the sort he really likes, which is very typical of a brother. I plan to buy him a packet of my favourite mints when it's his birthday. Granddad came around at lunchtime and in his hand he held a small gift-wrapped box. I was so excited; I thought I'll burst with happiness.

Of course I wouldn't have been so happy if I'd known what was going to happen.

"Open it up, sweet pea. It's your birthday gift."

Granddad handed me the gift box.

Despite knowing what it was, I enthusiastically ripped open the paper as my mum and brother watched. My obvious impatience seemed to please Granddad. I pulled open the box and the watch was beautiful, shiny and new with a colourful strap. I put it on my left wrist and held it at a distance to admire it once more. "It's lovely, Granddad." I ran around the table and gave him a big hug and a kiss on his cheek.

Granddad said, "Happy birthday, Ellie."

I smiled because nothing is more powerful than a birthday wish coming true. I said truthfully, "Awesome, it's just what I wanted it. You are so clever Granddad, you seem to know everything."

Granddad muttered, "Not everything, sweetheart. Not everything."

Jack asked Mother, "Can I go out on my bike? I promise to be back in time for the movie."

Mum hesitated before nodding her head but looked a little aggravated. "Don't be late, Jack. Four-thirty at the latest."

Jack nodded, turned and left the room. We heard the front door closing.

Granddad asked, "Any chance of a coffee?" He winked at me before sitting down at the table?

Mum quickly filled the kettle and plugged it in.

She said, "I've got some cake, for Ellie's birthday. Should we have some now?"

I took two cups out of the cupboard and put them next to the kettle. I could sense Granddad's excitement as he said, "I'd better get some cake, after all the money I've spent on that watch." He gave me another wink.

I fought an internal conflict between wanting to taste the cake and seeing Adam. The cake eventually lost as I reasoned it could wait. For effect, I groaned a little, "I need to go out, could we have the cake later, when Jack's back?"

"Where do you have to go on your birthday, young miss?" Granddad was feigning his funny policeman's voice.

I blinked and stammered, "To see someone, I'll be back real quick. I'll take the bike and we can all have a piece of cake before we go to the cinema."

I smiled triumphantly as Mummy said, "Don't be late; you heard what I said to Jack. I want today to be perfect, so get back here on time."

I felt my heart race as I nodded my head.

"Who are you going to see?" Granddad quizzed me again.

"Someone."

Granddad put his head to one side and looked at me suspiciously, "Someone?"

I replied quickly, "A friend, I want to show them my new watch and my gold medal."

Granddad retorted, "You shouldn't be going through the streets with all that gold around your neck, you might get attacked by pirates."

I quipped back, "It's not real gold, just looks like gold, besides my new coat will hide it."

Granddad asked mischievously, "What time is it?"

Unable to stop laughing, I looked at my new watch and replied, "Two-thirty."

"Back in two hours, otherwise no cake, birthday or not." Mum poured hot water into a cup. Instantly, the smell of coffee wafted around the room.

"I want another birthday hug from my granddaughter." Granddad's voice was tender.

I put on my new birthday coat and hugged him. Suddenly I felt an impulse to give my mummy one too. As I left I said, "Love you both."

Then I was gone.

Gone forever.

Chapter Eleven

My eyes sprang open and I thought maybe I'd just had a nightmare but it evaporated as I awoke. I lay there under my duvet, acclimatising myself as the early morning sun flooded the bedroom. Despite the sunshine, I felt something was wrong. It was the morning of Ellie's birthday and my copper's intuition was kicking in. The same way an animal senses a coming disaster like an earthquake.

I had a gut feeling, despite the welcoming sunshine, a calamity of some kind was on its way.

I showered and shaved and made a strong cup of coffee. It was black because I'd forgotten to get some milk. I was feeling down in the dumps, but happy at the same time. It was a strange, schizophrenic emotion, and I decided I needed a sugar rush to find some equilibrium, so I dropped four sugar lumps into my drink. My wife use to say life was like a sugar lump; it starts off symmetrical and sweet but eventually dissolves away until there's nothing left.

I drank the sweet coffee but the feeling of a coming tempest didn't go away.

Walking to the newsagent I bought a newspaper and a chocolate-flavoured croissant for breakfast. By the time I got back, the negative feeling started to abate, and once I was driving to Judy's house, later that day, I'd forgotten my foreboding.

It was my granddaughter's birthday. I was happy for her, what could go wrong?

"Thank you, Granddad," said Ellie with delight. She loved her present, although she'd already extracted from me what it was days before. She gave me a hug and a kiss on the cheek. I could smell vanilla on her, the sweet smell of childhood. She put the watch on her wrist and I noticed her gold medal hanging by a blue ribbon around her neck. I thought back to her last birthday and smiled to myself at how tall she'd grown in the twelve months. Through the kitchen window I could see the garden. Blackbirds were calling and sparrows darted in and out the copper beech hedge, while tits were on the feeder. The roses were possibly giving their last flush of the season. Sometimes, on summer nights, we use to watch the silent flight of bats as they hunted prey on the wing. This was a great house for children to grow up in.

Judy made me a cup of coffee and Jack went out on his bike.

Ellie asked if she could go out, too. Judy wasn't too happy and mentioned some birthday cake, but it was agreed Ellie should return by four-thirty so we could sit as a family eating the cake.

I asked Ellie whom she was meeting and her coyness suggested to me it might be a boy. Why do little girls grow up so quickly?

As she put on her coat, I announced, "I want another birthday hug off my granddaughter."

Ellie threw her head back as she laughed. I got my hug, so did her mother. She sounded excited as she headed for the door and said, "Love you both."

Then she was gone.

Judy offered me some lunch but I thought I'd save myself for the Chinese meal we would all have after the movie as part of Ellie's treat. My daughter informed me a truce seemed to exist in the office and her boss, Harry, now only spoke to her in a professional way. No small talk, just business. It seemed Jill had read him the riot act and it had worked.

I filled in the time reading a newspaper whilst Judy tidied up upstairs.

I hate tardiness, so when four-thirty came and the kids weren't home I felt slightly irritated. It was four-forty when Jack came in. His jeans were ripped and bloodied at the knee and he said he'd fallen off his bike. I asked him if he had seen his sister and he said no.

At five o'clock both Judy and I started to fret. This was so unlike Ellie who was usually so punctual. I needed to do something so I took Jack and we went scouting in my car. The tension formed knots in my neck. Like a cast-off kite in the wind, I was adrift with no idea which way to go; every road with no sign of her brought its own gloom and despair. Jack remained silent and my grip tightened on the steering wheel.

After about ten frantic minutes we saw some boys playing in a side road.

Jack pointed and gasped, "That's Ellie's bike!" One lad was doing wheelies on a bike too small for him. I slammed the brakes, screeching to a stop.

"Stay here, Jack." Leaving the car, I advanced towards the gang. There were six of them, aged from fourteen to seventeen. Regular fast food eaters, I thought.

The boy on the bike looked the oldest. I stormed up to him and grabbed his arm.

He snarled at me, like a feral animal. "What ya doin' man? Let go!"

The rest of his friends surrounded me, like moggies around a mouse.

I demanded, "Where did you get the bike from?"

The bike rider grandstanded in front of his mates. "What's it to do with you, like?"

I hissed back, "It's my granddaughter's."

"Can ya prove it, man?" Some of his friends nodded their heads and sneered in an aggressive way.

I hissed again through clenched teeth, "I tell you what bonny lad, you tell me where you got the bike and I'll let you walk home with both legs intact."

His mouth twisted with aggravation. "Oh, hard man are ya, granddad?"

My grip on his arm tightened like a vice and as his eyes looked down I head butted him. His head jerked back so far he looked in danger of snapping his spinal cord and blood rushed from his nose.

Leaving their bravado behind, his pals scampered down the avenue like scalded cats.

I said, "I'll ask you one more time, where did you get the bike?"

The look of surprise covered his face like a mask. He snorted, "Bloody 'ell, what ya do that for?"

I tightened my grip.

He yielded. "Okay, okay, we found it in Birchington Avenue. Tossed over, thought it had been abandoned."

I jerked my head to the side as I ordered him, "Get off."

He didn't need any more encouragement and he threw a leg over the seat and dismounted. Holding his bloody nose he ran after his friends. I opened the car boot and put the bike inside.

I sat down in the car and turning the ignition, said to Jack, "We're off to Birchington Avenue".

Ignoring the stunned stare coming from my grandson, I gripped the steering wheel hard as the tyres screamed away from the pavement.

It took us three minutes to reach Birchington Avenue, a street of middle-class houses with a parade of birch trees growing along the pavement. Fear froze my blood and I wanted to scream. Apart from a few parked cars and a black cat wandering down the pavement, the avenue was empty.

I turned to Jack, "This is only five minutes from your house. Do any of Ellie's friends live here?"

"I don't know." Jack sounded miserable.

"If her bike was abandoned, something must have happened to her."

I spun the car around and headed back to the house.

Judy was waiting at the gate, arms flapping and I knew by her expression, Ellie hadn't come home.

"We've found her bike," I informed her as I entered the house. Picking up the phone, I said to Judy. "The police usually don't get excited over a missing person until twenty-four hours have passed, but with Ellie's age and the dumped bike, hopefully they'll react immediately."

I heard her sob as I dialled 999.

After ten minutes a patrol car came over. Two bobbies, one looking as if he hadn't yet started shaving, took details. Then a second police car turned up. Using a radio, a policewoman from the second car sent out a description of Ellie. By five-thirty, an all-points bulletin went out and our lives changed forever.

By ten-thirty, darkness and despair covered the house. A medical officer gave Judy an injection to help her get over her hysterics and I put Jack to bed. The poor kid was beside himself, and I had to wipe away his tears and snot before he eventually settled down. By midnight and in the darkness of the garden, I furtively threw the birthday cake into the bin. The pain behind my eyes felt as if they had been slashed by a razor. My heart twisted like a tourniquet and I struggled not to have a blackout.

I knew by then, of course, Ellie wasn't coming home.

Jill Adams came around next day with a plain-clothes junior officer.

"Tony, I've asked to be made officer in charge, and we're going to treat this as a missing person with possibility of abduction. That way we can quickly get the necessary resources on the case."

I stood in the kitchen. Jack sat at the table and Judy was still in bed, medicated.

Jill continued, "Hell's teeth, Tony, you look like death, did you get any sleep last night?"

"What do you think?"

She looked apologetic. "I'm sorry." She turned to her colleague. "This is DC Sweetman. He's here to help." He looked in his late thirties, with a short haircut.

I said, "There's been no ransom demand, besides the family's not rich, so we have to work on the motive not being money. That leaves only sex. Have we let any paedophiles out from Durham in the last few weeks?"

Jill looked despondent. "Tony, I know this is hard for you, but you're not on the case. You have to let us do our job."

I thought DC Sweetman couldn't solve a game of Cluedo, but kept my toxic thoughts to myself. My heart was racing and a migraine split my head.

Jill informed us, "We've got twenty officers doing door to door and someone at the station is talking to local radio and TV. We'll have Ellie's picture all over the media.

DC Sweetman said, "If you have a recent picture of the girl, it would help."

Jill corrected him. "Her name's Ellie. Mr Bell will cooperate, but if we're going to treat this case as a possible abduction," she turned to me, "you know what the first major step is don't you, Tony?"

"Eliminate from your enquiry the family."

"Yes."

"That means you want to do a forensic search of the house."

"I'm afraid so, Tony."

"Wait until Judy gets up. I'll take her out whilst your dust squad go over the house."

I took Judy out in the car, using the pretence of searching for Ellie. It would keep her mind occupied. Jack elected to stay at home and as we left, four forensic officers, carrying cases and dressed in white overalls, entered the house. We had to drive past a small crowd of neighbours; they looked as bereft as we felt. We heard on the local radio station about Ellie and at the end of the bulletin, I switched it off. We saw some of the police doing their door-to-door and as we passed the allotments, officers were looking in the sheds.

I said to my daughter, "I think Ellie was visiting a boy."

She surprised me when she replied, "I believe his name is Adam."

Judy didn't know exactly Adam's address, but she knew enough for me to use my detective skills and ask around. We found the house in a street of ornate Victorian houses complete with sash windows. Adam's house had a white fence and was double fronted with a large blue door at the end of a long path. I knocked and his mother came to the door. She recognised Judy immediately and, gasping, fought hard not to break down.

"Please come on in." The house was neat and tidy and she showed us into a sitting room with a big bay window. A vase of flowers was on a side table and her husband walked in and invited us to sit down.

I said, "I'm, sorry to disturb you, but our Ellie has gone missing. We believe she may have been on her way over here. We have to ask, did she call yesterday?"

Both shook their heads and the mother said, "Was she coming to visit our son, Adam? He's just come out of hospital; I guess your girl was coming to see him."

I asked, "Has she been here before?"

Adam's father said, "No, not as far as we know."

His wife nodded her head in agreement. She asked, "Would you like a cup of tea?"

We nodded and she disappeared to the kitchen.

"I'm sure she'll turn up safe. Teenagers, eh?" said the father. "It's always a drama with them."

Judy sniffed, "Ellie is only just twelve."

"I'm sorry; it's just that I'm saying, you have to be optimistic, early days yet."

We sat in silence waiting for the tea.

Adam's mother came in with a tray and four china cups and a pot of tea. She poured out the drink.

She said to Judy, "Adam's never mentioned your daughter, are they class mates?"

"No, I think Adam's in a year above her. I think she may have been a little sweet on him, you know how girls are."

"In some ways, I'm glad we only have a son, although I think both sexes are trouble in their own way."

Her husband asked, "Should we make a statement to the police?"

I replied, "No, I don't think that's necessary." I finished my cup and stood up. "Judy and I thank you for your time, I hope Adam's back on his feet quickly." I turned to my daughter, "Judy, I think we need to get home."

We drove off with their kind thoughts ringing in our ears. When we arrived back at the house, the crowd had got bigger and there were a few press photographers hanging around.

Jill was standing in the front garden with a forensic officer. Next to her stood young Jack, his face grey as a tomb stone.

Jill walked towards me urgently. "Tony, we've found something."

Chapter Twelve

I wheeled my bike through our gate. It would take about ten
minutes to reach Adam's hous. As I peddled away; I was
unaware of a white van pulling out from the kerb and
following me down the road. I was in a world of my own. I
hummed the song God Only Knows:

*I was on my way to be kissed, I was excited, I mean, I was
really excited!*

My smile couldn't have been wider.

*Five minutes of pushing the pedals, and I was cycling
down an avenue of trees when I passed by a parked, small
white van. A man with a hood and with his arm in a sling
was trying to lift a collie dog into the back. It was obvious that
with his injured arm he was having trouble. As I passed I
heard his voice, "Can you help me, Ellie?"*

*The dog looked like Lassie from the movies; I circled
around and parked my bike against a tree. I should have found
it odd that a stranger would know my name, but my head was
too full of the things I was going to say to Adam. The man was*

bent over, and with his hood I couldn't see his face as I stood next to him. Bending down, I lifted the dog and pushed it into the van. At the same time I felt a violent push in my back and found myself following the dog. My feet were off the ground and my shins scuffed against the van as I landed heavily, face down on the metal floor. Before I could scream a rag was pushed over my mouth. It tasted bitter and smelled of chemicals. Next thing, I passed out.

When I opened my eyes, I couldn't focus. It was cold and dark everywhere, and as my eyes acclimatised I could see I was in a shed, a type of wooden garden hut. My muscles hurt and I had a dreadful headache. I saw an unopened can of Coke beside me, and flipping open the tab I drank half of it in one go. Taking a deep breath, I burped and quickly finished off the drink. Standing up, I looked down and gasped in shock. I was still wearing my new top coat, but underneath my clothes were changed. I was in a dress very similar to the one I wore when I won the gold medal. Same turquoise colour and made of velvet but a little tight. It was similar but not exact. Feeling confused, I looked at my feet and saw that my shoes had been replaced with white velvet slippers. The overcoat, I guessed, was supplied because there was no heating in the hut. I looked at my wrist; my new watch was gone as was my gold medal.

I tried the door and wasn't surprised to find it was locked. Going to a dirty window, I wiped a porthole in the grime. I couldn't see much, but it looked as if I was inside an abandoned industrial warehouse with a high ceiling. I could see a set of gym weights and an empty bench press. A tape played on a loop in the warehouse; it was the Beach Boys' God Only Knows.

I stood back from the window and looked around my wooden cell. Apart from a chair and bucket, a mattress and some blankets were strewn on the floor. I walked over to the chair and then I realised something. I stopped and ignoring my heaving chest and panting breath, gingerly put my right hand down to the hem of the skirt. I went under the dress and confirmed what I feared.

I'd been stripped of my knickers.

I fell onto the mattress and brought my knees up to my chest. Lying like a foetus, hands to my mouth, I screamed with terror and then I screamed again and continued screaming.

I wanted my mummy.

I have no idea how long I lay on the mattress, but I was suddenly aware of the ceiling lights going on in the warehouse. I heard footsteps, slow and menacing, and a dog barking. Then came the sound of a wooden bar being lifted and the cabin door squeaking on dry hinges. I sat up, terrified; my blood ran like ice, my nails bit into the flesh of my hand as I screwed up my fists.

The door opened and I gasped.

Standing there was Darth Vader.

Actually, it wasn't Darth Vader; it was someone wearing a Darth Vader mask. I knew he wasn't Darth because, whilst he was tall and well built, he wasn't tall enough.

I was mystified and terrified at the same time.

The figure said, "Hello, Ellie. Welcome to the dark side."

The man's voice sounded just like the movie because he was using something called a voice changer. I could see the dog some distance behind him. Its tail and ears were down and I knew the animal was as scared of its owner as I was.

Darth Vader continued, "Today will be a day to remember for I have longed to look into your eyes."

I spat out, "My granddad will find me."

"There is no Luke Skywalker or Obi-Wan to save you. Your father is dead and your granddad's a fool."

I said in a loud voice and pointed, my outstretched hand trembling. "If you don't let me go home, you'll be in real trouble and my granddad is not a fool, he's a policeman."

The man let out a mechanical laugh. "Ellie, you haven't been harmed, yet. But soon you'll want to come to the dark side; hunger will make you beg like a dog. I won't take you by force, I'll only take you when you plead and are ready, then you and I will be one and I will make you a woman. Meanwhile, you will stay here and starve but when you are ready, you will lie down for the Master. For now, I bid you farewell, young Ellie."

The lights went out and I found myself in the murky dark. I put my hand into my coat pocket and felt the bar of chocolate. It was my brother's birthday gift.

Ignoring the tears running down my cheeks, I whispered, "Thank you, Jack."

Chapter Thirteen

In the kitchen, Jill showed me a see-through, plastic bag. It measured four inches by four inches and I could see immediately what it inside it.

Jill looked embarrassed as she said, "We found this behind the bath panel. I think you know what it is."

"I know what it is, cannabis. Bloody pot. "I gave Jack an angry look and demanded, "Is it yours?"

Jack confirmed with an apology. With his head bent and eyes looking at the floor he said, "Sorry, Granddad."

I stared at him whilst I heard Jill say, "Look this has nothing to do with the investigation. I'll take it back to the station, but I suggest you have word with your grandson."

I grabbed Jack by the shoulder and frogmarched him into the garden.

I yelled, "Bloody drugs, bloody drugs after all I've told you!" I pointed to my head with a finger. "They poison the mind, Jack. I don't want a member of my family a pot head." I raised my voice even higher, "Do you understand?"

Jack shook his head in a remorseful manner. "I promise I'll never take it again."

I was angry and made no attempt to conceal the fact. "This shit kills, Jack. Maybe not in the traditional sense, but it kills ambition. I've seen too much not to understand the damage it does. Young kids, minds burnt out, never going to recover, never." I paused before asking, "Who's your supplier?"

Jack looked at the ground.

I repeated, "Who's your supplier, Jack?"

He paused for a moment before confessing, "A biker called Tomlinson; he supplies most of the kids around here. I don't know his other name, he rides a Harley."

"Do you promise you'll never use this shit again?"

"I promise, Granddad. I'm really sorry. At the time, it felt like a laugh, all my mates are doing it. But I'm going to change. Granddad, honestly, I'm really going to change, change for the better."

I probed, "In what way son?"

He answered contritely. "Since Ellie disappeared, I realised I've been a rotten brother. When she comes home again, I'm really going to be nice to her." He started to weep. "I really miss my sister."

I guess you only appreciate what you have after it's gone. I couldn't bring myself to ask him what if Ellie didn't come home. I let hope rest where it could.

In my late wife's favourite book, *Anna Karenina*, Tolstoy wrote every family is unhappy in its own way. Perhaps I'd been trying so hard to make things right, I sometimes missed what was under my nose. I may be guilty, who knows? Bloody families; they are all alike, bloody hard work and a mystery.

I put my arm around Jack and whispered, "I believe you, son. I believe you."

★★★★

"Are you out of your fucking mind?" Webster quickly turned to Jill and said unconvincingly, "Sorry about the swearing, love."

The three of us were in his office. Webster sat at his desk with a mug of tea resting on some papers. He had put on weight and lost more hair.

Jill and I stood like two kids in the principal's office.

He looked at me, "Flipping heck, Tony, there's no way I can have a civilian on the team."

I replied with a calm voice. "I'm not a civilian. I'm a retired detective and a good one if you can remember that far back."

Webster looked exasperated. "You're still an effing civilian. Okay you look the same, despite it being years since you buggered off, but the Chief Constable will have my balls for breakfast if he finds out."

Jill leaned forward and said reassuringly, "There is a way, sir."

Webster asked frantically, "How can there be a way?"

"Well, I'm the lead detective and as you know I'm going through an acrimonious divorce…"

Webster cut her short, "Don't tell me about those, I've had two of my own."

Jill charmed him with a smile. "Well you'll know, sir, it can be difficult to give one hundred per cent with a busy background, and the Chief Constable will want a quick result on this one, seeing it's all in the papers."

Webster shook his head like a dog fussing over a bone. "Well?"

"We could bring Tony in as a consultant. I believe it's been done before."

Webster's eyebrows shot up. "I can't afford a fucking consultant. My budgets are getting cut."

I retorted, "I'll be free. I won't even charge expenses."

Webster sat back in his leather chair and brought his cupped hand to his chin. "Mother me bairn, if this goes wrong my whole career will go up in smoke."

I reassured him. "It won't go wrong, the quicker we solve this the quicker your blood pressure will come down."

"I'll have to have a contract drawn up and duly signed."

I confirmed, "Not a problem."

As the last brick in Webster's defence wall fell away he said, "Okay then, you're back on the team, Tony."

He scratched his head, not believing what he'd just agreed to.

Jill couldn't contain the smug look as we turned towards the door.

Webster's voice followed us out of the room as he boomed, "One more thing, Tony, remember you're only a consultant. That means DS Adams is Batman and you're just fucking Robin."

As we walked down the passage, Jill whispered to me, "He called me love and little old me thought the dinosaurs had died out."

I replied, "Surprising how high an empty balloon can fly."

My new partner allowed a thin smile to cross her lips.

So now I had something to occupy my mind. I ignored the twist of tension in my chest. Tears in my eyes, I closed them and willed myself to think of nothing but the job in hand. I wanted to feel nothing. I wanted to feel nothing at all.

From the station we drove in an unmarked car to Birchington Avenue.

Jill informed me as she drove, "A Mrs Tomkinson reported in. She may have seen something."

We knocked at number 27. A woman, heavily pregnant and aged about the same as the number of the house, answered the door.

Jill asked, "Mrs Tomkinson?"

The woman corrected her. "Tomlinson. Are you the police?"

Jill nodded.

"Come on in." It seemed she was expecting us.

The woman's left eye was closed and the side of her face was bruised black and blue. Three fingers were taped together, suggesting at least one was broken. The woman noticed us staring at her injuries and said, "Fell down the stairs." She touched her swollen belly. "The baby's okay, the doctor came and checked." She smiled at us, trying to put a good spin on the statement. She indicated we should sit on the sofa and looked nervous. I thought she looked drained of any self-esteem.

Jill said, "Nice house."

I suspected Jill was curious how this woman could afford such a house in this street.

The woman laughed without humour. "We don't own it, we're only renters. We get help from the social."

Jill introduced herself. "My name is DS Adams and this is…" She paused with her empty, upturned hand suspended in mid-air. She obviously hadn't thought this bit through. She brought her hand back, scratched her eyebrow and concluded, "This is Tony Bell. I understand you may have some information on the disappearance of Ellie Peach."

"It's not much really. I saw a small white van on the day the young girl disappeared and after it left I saw a girl's bike parked against the tree, the one just outside the house. Later the bike disappeared; I think some boys may have taken it. I thought it strange that whoever owned it hadn't come back for it."

I asked urgently, "Anything else, you didn't by chance take down the registration number of the van?"

"No I'm sorry. I'm sure I haven't been a help at all."

Jill declared, "No actually, that's been a great help." She stood up, "Thank you so much."

I stood up and peered at a framed photograph on the mantelpiece. "Is this your husband?" He looked like a younger version of Jerry Garcia.

She said quietly, "Yes."

"I'm not an expert, but is that a Harley-Davidson he's sitting on?"

The woman wrapped her arms around herself. "Oh yes, it's his love and joy."

I smiled at her, "Not many Harleys in this part of the world."

The woman stayed at the door watching us walk to the car. Suddenly I informed Jill, "Forgotten my pen." I turned quickly and went back towards the house. Jill stood at the car, one hand on the roof and keys in the other. As I approached the door, I gently held the woman on the shoulder and led her inside.

In the hallway I turned her around and asked urgently, "He did this, your husband, didn't he?" I indicated to her injuries.

The suddenness of my question lowered her resistance and before she could lie, tears emerged as she nodded her head. She'd fooled the doctor, but she wasn't fooling me.

I demanded, "Where is he now?"

The woman had no more lies to give. "Drinking with his pals at the Tyne Dock," she said.

In the car, I said, "Looks like we're looking for a white van."

Jill thoughtfully replied, "I bet he's a right slime ball, her husband. 'Fell down the stairs', my arse."

I reminded her, "Jill you've got to stay focused, what's next?"

She shook her head. "I don't know, Boy Wonder." She gave a sigh, "Batman's all out of ideas."

I paused for a moment, gathering my thoughts. I suppressed the emotions of a granddad with a missing grandchild and stayed focused on the job in hand. I eventually said, "What we need is the word from the street. We need a Huggy Bear."

"What's a Huggy Bear?"

"He was in that cop programme on TV. Huggy Bear was the street-wise informant."

"Oh him! Where will we find a wise-cracking, black American in this town?"

"Well, I know a guy. He ain't American nor is he black, but I think I know where he is right now."

She turned her head and looked at me. "Yeah, where?"

"Drive the bat mobile to the Tyne Dock pub, Wonder Woman."

Jill shook her head. "You're not very good playing this game are you?"

Our journey would take us ten minutes. Whilst I was wise cracking or focusing on the job, the pain of Ellie's disappearance went into remission. However, as soon as my mind was off the inquiry the pain returned. I'd been bereft when my wife died and the hurt was unbearable. Death of a loved one is terrible but losing a child, a younger member of the family; the pain turns septic, it burns like battery acid in the pit of your stomach and eats away at you like a cancer. It was three days now since Ellie disappeared, with every minute the hope of finding her alive fell through the hourglass. The police, running around like headless chickens, had arranged an appeal for the TV stations. I said I would do it, but Judy insisted she, as the mother, should do it. She appealed on camera for any information, no matter how small, to be brought forward. I knew it was a futile gesture, but it gave the appearance of doing something.

I sat in the car festering in my own misery as Jill drove. I looked out the car window and mouthed to the passing wind, "Where are you, sweet pea?"

Jill sensed my anguish. She asked softly, "How you doing, Tony?"

I sighed, "Not too well. If I think of it, I fear I might break down. I need to keep my mind occupied; otherwise I'm going to land in the loony bin." I turned towards her as we slowed down for a traffic light. "Ask me something."

"What do you mean?"

"Anything, just keep me talking, help me keep my mind off the bloody awful scenarios of what might have happened to poor Ellie."

Jill asked quickly. "How old are you, Tony?"

"Fifty-eight."

She shrugged. "You look younger. How long have you been retired?"

I replied, "Coming up twelve years."

She asked me incredulously. "So tell me, how the hell did you manage to retire so young? You went before the rules allow."

I gave a sardonic grin. "It was a medical retirement; seems I was no longer fit for the job."

"Bloody hell, what did you have?"

"Tinnitus."

"Tinnitus?"

"Yes, it's an infection that affects the ears."

"I know what it is," she sighed. "And that made you medically unfit for duty?"

"You can't have alarm bells going off in your head. Not when you're a copper. I wouldn't be able to distinguish the difference between sirens."

"And I guess Tinnitus is hard to disprove."

"That's what Miss Donaldson told me."

"Who's Miss Donaldson?"

"She was head of HR at the time."

"You're something, Tony. For the sake of our new partnership, I'm going to assume your medical discharge was genuine."

"Or what?"

"I would have to arrest you for, I don't know, something!"

I pointed to the side of the road. "Park up here, we've arrived. The pub is just there."

Tyne Dock public house was a Victorian drinking house built for the shipyard workers. Basic in design and with a red brick façade, it was on its last legs now the shipyards were closed.

I said to Jill, "I suggest you stay here. When the last woman walked through its doors, King Edward was still on the throne."

"Tony, I'm the lead detective. We should go in together."

"Seriously Jill, if the informant is in there, he's not going to talk to a serving officer, especially a female one."

She sighed deeply. "You do know women have the vote, right?"

"I know we have to do what we can to find Ellie."

"How are your ears?"

I lied, "A little ringing noise, nothing much."

"If you're not out in ten minutes, I'm coming in. Okay?"

"Okay."

I left Jill in the driver's seat. As I passed the small courtyard on the side of the building, I saw six motorbikes parked up. One was a Harley.

I pushed open the door and entered. The interior was tired and looked like it was still the original décor.

I saw the leather-clad bikers sitting around a table in a corner. I recognised the Harley owner, the wife basher and drug supplier to school kids. The average age of the gang was early thirties, all too dim to light up a chandelier. Three had shaved heads, two wore long, messy hair to their shoulders and the Harley owner had a ponytail. All had various tattoos as well as decorative metal rings hanging from their ears. All were ugly and I guess none of them ever flossed their teeth. I walked over and stood to the left of Tomlinson and addressed them. "I'm looking for a biker named Tomlinson."

I sensed him looking up as he lethargically asked, "Who wants to know?"

They stopped playing their card game and looked me up and down. All of them were heavier than me. One had the words HATE and LOVE tattooed on his knuckles, while another had a flag of Saint George on his neck.

I furtively spread my feet and lowered my centre of gravity then replied in a relaxed voice, "I have a message from his wife."

The Harley owner put his hands on the table and pushed himself up, whilst asking, "How the fuck do you know my wife?"

Before he was half way up, I swung my right hand through an arc, chopping him in the throat, like an axe sinking deep into a tree trunk. I drove my hand beyond skin, forcing his Adam's apple through his windpipe. Stunned, he grabbed his throat, choking and throwing spit into the air, trying to find the reflex that would allow air to pass again down to his lungs. His eyes were bulging and I knew he would be feeling as if he was drowning. Before anybody else moved I smashed my fist and knuckles into his nose. Bone, blood and gristle flew out and he dropped deadweight, taking a few glasses of beer with him to the floor. The rest of the gorillas were up on their feet, trying to understand what had just happened.

A long silence followed.

I'd just beaten up the silverback and they were clueless and leaderless.

Eventually, the Hate and Love guy grunted, "What was the message?"

It was my turn to feel confused. I turned to him. "What?"

The thicko said, "You said you had a message from his wife."

I shrugged, paused then replied, "Oh, tell him not to be late for his tea."

"Oh." The thicko nodded his head wisely to the others as if he was experiencing an Epiphany. They nodded back.

I turned around and left.

Outside, Jill was checking her face in a mirror case. As I sat down she asked, "Anything?"

I shook my head, "Nothing that can help Ellie."

The evening was cool and crisp when I arrived at Judy's just after eight. Jack was sitting in the kitchen chatting quietly to a young girl. Family photos were spread randomly on the table. I could hear Judy in the sitting room whispering, I assumed, to the girl's mother.

Jack turned to me. Sounding melancholy he said, "Hello, Granddad. This is Talia, Ellie's friend."

I could see Talia had been crying and realised Jack had been comforting her. I recognised he had grown up a lot in the last few days. He was no longer the stroppy teenager he had been. A shadow of sadness covered his eyes; he was still waiting for his sister to return home.

He half smiled and then blinked twice in succession. "Do you want a cup of tea, Granddad?"

I shook my head.

He asked, "Any news about Ellie?"

I shook my head again and said softly, "The police are doing everything they can, Jack."

The girl said, "I haven't slept a wink since Ellie disappeared."

I smiled warmly, "None of us have. It's a terrible time. It's the not knowing that eats away at you." I let the silence stretch. "Have you all eaten?"

The two wearily nodded.

I realised our world had crashed and with it the landscape and rules had changed forever. Even our language had changed; we tip-toed around, desperate not to say the wrong thing, not wanting to be clumsy and add more distress. Ellie's disappearance had left a huge gap in our lives and in our hearts. We were like a defeated army, retreating from an invisible enemy, feeling weary and battle fatigued.

The day before, the local vicar had come around to offer solace but we're not a religious family. That's not to say we were without any spiritual elements, but we found succour in the family unit, not in the church congregation. I was the shepherd, the family my flock and I'd committed the ultimate sin of losing our little lamb. The guilt soured in my bones, the remorse marinated my brain. To stop myself breaking down, I started singing *God Only Knows* in my head, hoping the words would drive away my darkest thoughts.

The song vaguely blocked out for a moment the sound of murder, a bone breaking, a little girl screaming a helpless scream. The sound of violent rape and tearing of young flesh, the last thing she would hear, the grunting of a pervert biting like a rabid dog, an angel fighting for her life, the awful sound of a young life being snuffed out. The scenes were just too awful. I concentrated on the song although I could hardly breathe.

The two others stared into space, each lost in their own world of sorrow.

Eventually Jack asked, "Are you all right, Granddad?"

I choked. "Not really, son. It's difficult for all of us."

Jack got up from his chair and came to me. He was nearly the same height as me. He put his arms around my neck and hugged me. "I love you, Granddad." A shy Talia walked across, not sure if she was welcome. Her lower lip trembled slightly. I opened my arm and brought her into the embrace. Then as the three of us hugged, we all sobbed.

Chapter Fourteen

I screamed with hunger. I screamed with thirst, but most of all I screamed with absolute terror.

Darth Vader would creep in each day, to mock and ask if I was ready. For effect he would always play the music on the recorder. I sensed he was getting a little impatient, although he continued enjoying having power over me. My blood froze and my flesh crawled with every visit. I knew he was cruel to his dog and he wouldn't hesitate to be cruel to me. But every hour I resisted gave Granddad the opportunity to find me.

I finished Jack's chocolate bar on the first day. The second day I felt faint with hunger and the stomach pains cramped me up. I longed for my mum's cooking, steak and salad. My mouth watered at the thought of KFC with the grease running down my fingers and the over-salted chips. But by the fourth day my body seemed to have got use to the idea I wasn't going to eat. I didn't understand my body was eating its own reserves, my fats and then my muscles. A viper can live six months without food; how long can a little girl live?

My dress was now baggy on me. Occasionally, my jailer would give me a can of Coke. I would drink it greedily all in one go and disappoint myself by not rationing it. I decided I would rather die of hunger than be molested by this monster. It would cost me a great deal in self-control, but I would not submit.

I fantasised I could gorge his eyes out and run away as he collapsed into a pool of blood. Once, when I fell into a shallow sleep, I had a nightmare in which he kissed me. He put his filthy wet mouth on my lips and his breath smelled of rotten meat. As I squirmed under his brutal embrace I ripped his tongue out with my virgin white teeth. I started running away, but in this lurid dream, no matter how fast I ran, I couldn't escape the hand of the bloodied monster. Soaked in cold sweat, I woke up screaming.

I then planned my real escape.

There were three empty Coke cans on the hut floor. In frustration I stamped on one. As the can crushed I felt better, so I crushed all three and that's when I got my idea. I continued stamping on one can until it was flattened and ignoring the ache in my foot, picked up the aluminium can. Granddad used to play a game with us. Taking a wire paper clip, he would ask Jack and I to be creative and think of all the different ways you could use a paperclip. When we'd exhausted all the possible answers he would straighten the clip so it was just a long piece of wire. He would urge us to think further, and of course we now saw the clip in a different way and would add many more uses to our list. He called it 'creative thinking' or 'thinking outside the box'.

I looked at my crushed can and saw a pliable piece of aluminium and an opportunity. I flattened all three cans and with two, using the edge of an arm of the chair as a fulcrum, folded over two leading edges to create a point. I spent a long time bending the creases until the metal tore, exposing a jagged edge. Ignoring my blistered and cut fingers, I put the two cans together and rolled them to form a pencil with a sharp point. I wrapped the third can around to stabilise the original two and create a hilt. I looked at my finished product. It didn't look pretty, but I held in my hand a rather crude knife. It would be no good for putting butter on toast, nor was it as sharp as a scalpel, but it was ideal for stabbing. For the first time since my abduction and crazy with hunger, I smiled.

This viper had just got its fangs.

I lay wakeful in the half darkness of the hut. I held my weapon in my hand and fantasised how I would do it. Hunger was making me think like a wild animal, cornered and dangerous. Granddad once told me about a drug the body produces when you are in a frightening situation. He said it helped you fight or flee. Adrenaline now flowed like a river through my body. Jimmy, my coach, taught me breathing techniques to calm myself before a competition. I lay and took slow deliberate breaths, forcing my racing heart to slow down. The ogre wore a plastic hood, which acted like a helmet, protecting his head from attack. Like opening an oyster, I had to find the soft spot to put the knife in to open up this particular mollusc.

I heard the outer door slide open and the lights came on.

My troll had arrived.

The footsteps echoed around the warehouse as they came closer. Taking a deep breath, I stood up, casting off my coat, holding my hands by my side, concealing my weapon. I could hear the dog sniffing at the door as Brian Wilson's song vibrated once more around the cathedral-sized warehouse.

I could sense him on the other side of the door before it creaked open and I saw the fiend with his Darth Vader mask.

My insides shaking, my voice croaked, "I'm ready, Master."

He didn't move. He seemed surprised so he just stood motionless at the doorway. Who knows what goes through the mind of a pervert, a power game-playing, dirty brute.

All that followed was a terrifying silence.

I had been prepared for him to rush at me, but he didn't. I could hear his breathing through his voice changer. Magnified and getting faster, it was the unmistakable sound of a beast, an aroused monster. I feared if he didn't move soon, I would pass out and he would have his way with me while I was unconscious.

I repeated, "I'm ready." The words hardly escaped passed my dry lips.

His breathing had a strange wild sound and he replied with a mechanical voice. "I've waited a long time, Ellie. It's not that I need to do this, I HAVE to. You see, I have no control over my desire. Wanting you is as natural as nature; in fact it is my nature. I don't want you to be scared. You are not my first little girl, but you are the most beautiful. That is why I wanted you to gift me this treasure, your body." He took a step forward. "I'll try not to hurt you, Ellie, but you know what they say, you can't play with a butterfly without damaging its delicate wings."

He moved towards me. It would take three steps; I gripped my DIY knife tighter.

"Hello Ellie," the voice lisped menacingly behind the mask. "Now we're going to have some fun."

I screamed as I thrust the knife towards his crotch but his hands were agile and he was alert. He grunted and managed to block my arm. The move took me by surprise and I punched empty air. I had messed up my opportunity. He grabbed me by the throat with his big hands and I realised he hadn't seen the weapon, didn't know I was armed.

He sounded angry. "Why have you spoilt it? You're just like all the others after all."

My feet left the ground. God, he was strong. I writhed frantically. I was choking, gagging for air, my head spinning and I felt dizzy. I stabbed again, then again and again, each time the knife went into the flesh, ripping the top of his thigh.

"You bitch!" He dropped me as he pulled at the makeshift knife that was deep in his leg and I was through his legs like a ferret, heading for the door. "Oh, no you don't." He spat through his teeth as he turned and gave chase.

I ran into the warehouse, my footsteps echoing around the empty building. The Beach Boys had stopped singing and there was another problem. The dog thought I was playing a game and ran with me barking. Suddenly she was under my feet and I tumbled to the floor. I could hear my abductor's footsteps. I quickly picked myself up, but I was now disorientated.

Where was the door?

Darth Vader's helmet seemed to be an impediment to his running, and hopefully the gored leg was giving him hell. I ran but in my confusion, realised I was running deeper into the warehouse. I could hear him panting behind me, the dog continued with its playful barking and I screamed as I ran for my life.

I saw a double door with a bar across. There was a mouldy sign that read 'Emergency Exit'. Just what I needed, an emergency exit! His footsteps were so close behind me that I thought I could feel his rotten breath on my neck. I ran towards the door and prayed it wasn't padlocked. Arms outstretched I ran into the bar and the doors flew opened.

The force of the storm struck me. I was outside, it was night and a tempest raged all around. Within seconds I was drenched with rain and I realised I was a stone's throw from the river. I could see the lights of the buildings on the other side; this side seemed to be in darkness. I looked behind me; my abductor had thrown off his mask and was limping through the emergency exit. In the dark I couldn't see his face, but I sensed the anger that twisted his features.

Which way to run, please help me someone, which way?

I screamed again and ran into the darkness.

Chapter Fifteen

It was two o'clock in the morning; the lonely hour. Despite my thumping stress headache, I nursed a neat whisky in my hand four fingers deep. With each mouthful, it felt as if the four fingers were down my throat. Four days and no sign of Ellie, the chances of finding her alive now required a divine intervention. I wasn't hopeful. I closed my eyes and went once more over the facts. A possible sighting of a white van; how many white vans are there? It was a labyrinth of dead ends and false leads although Jill, bless her, had DC Sweetman going through a long list and cross referencing possible connections. My knuckles were bruised from hitting the biker. Hopefully he was no longer battering his wife. Smashing his ugly face had been a sort of cathartic release and a punishment for supplying drugs to kids, but I still felt depressed. The thought in my head kept going around in a loop, how do you kidnap a young girl in broad daylight and disappear? I threw back my head and drained my glass, the amber liquid burning my throat.

I thought about what the law would do if they ever caught Ellie's abductor. I'd worked in the warped ethos of a dripping wet criminal justice system where the criminals are considered the victims. It's like looking at justice through Alice's looking glass. Everything is backwards; too many mad March hares wearing wigs sit in our courts. The law was definitely getting soft. When I was a cop I carried handcuffs not hankies. Nowadays, just to get a promotion, you have to be a broccoli-eating vegetarian.

That's why it was easy to leave. I'm not even sure, despite having an excellent record, I could even get a job on the police force today. No room on the thin blue line for a meat- and-two-veg man.

Then there was my daughter. She was a victim of the system too. I had been away too often chasing the bad guys. We did climb rainbows sometimes, especially when I took her to the local swimming pool. I taught her to swim and she represented her school at the town's swimming gala. I tried my best, but sometimes, I just know it wasn't good enough. They don't teach that at the police cadet school. My wife and I tried for years for a second child, but it wasn't to be. Ellie, my wife, joked and said it was because my police uniform trousers were too tight.

I miss my wife; sometimes I miss her like a severed limb.

I tried reading; I had a large collection of books, all of them about history. I loved the subject, especially

WWI and the battle of the Somme. My grandfather died on the first day, a lion led by donkeys. My dad was only a boy when he lost his father. I never knew my granddad, of course, which was something I regretted very much and I compensated by reading as much as I could about the war. It seemed a way of respecting his memory. When I was sixteen, my dad took me to France to see the grave.

I've promised Judy I would take her one day.

Slowly I came to the conclusion my mind was too full of chatter to concentrate on a book. I filled up my whisky glass again and lifted up the telephone, holding a piece of paper. I inhaled slowly, exhaled again. I dialled the number written on the paper. The phone rang three times and was answered.

"Hello, you're through to the Samaritans, how can I help you?"

The voice was female, gentle and friendly. I stayed silent. I just wanted to hear a voice that belonged to a good person, some stranger who didn't share my pain and had never met Ellie.

The voice repeated, "You're through to the Samaritans. Can I help you?" The voice remained kind.

I remained silent.

I heard her voice down the telephone, "You need only talk when you want to. If you don't want to say anything, that's okay, too."

I was conscious of my breathing.

The female voice waited before almost whispering, "You can tell me anything you want. The call is confidential. Only I will hear and nothing is recorded."

I stayed dumb and my mouth felt as if I'd been chewing on cuttlefish.

The female now was quiet until eventually she breathed, "My name's Jenny, do you have a name?"

Her voice had a sweet resonance and I heard myself answering, "Tony."

"How can I help you, Tony?"

I sighed, "You can't."

She asked softly, "Are you suicidal?"

I replied, "No."

"Depressed?"

"No, not depressed."

"So how do you feel, Tony?"

"I feel, well, I guess the feeling's guilt."

"What do you feel guilty about, Tony?"

My stomach twisted as I cried out, "I've let my family down."

I slept through my alarm so was surprised when the telephone woke me up. I leapt out of bed. The stubble on my chin felt parasitic, while the pain from my throat was as if someone had slammed a beer glass down and stamped on it.

I lifted up the receiver, "Hello."

"Tony?" It was Jill's voice.

"Yes?"

"Can you come straight down to the station? I've sent a patrol car to pick you up, should be with you in a few minutes."

"What's happened?"

"We've found a body."

Chapter Sixteen

*I*nto the storm I ran. The driving rain was making me blind as it washed away my tears, but I also knew the rain would be to my advantage, making it harder for the monster to find me. It seemed I was in an unused industrial area, and as I ran I could see big, dark walls towering above me. Where was the exit?

I had run from one rat trap into another. I realised it was an abandoned shipyard and as I rushed I decided to head towards the sound of the river. There had to be an escape route there, another emergency exit.

I could hear my abductor shouting and the dog barking.

Suppressing the urge to scream I kept running into the night shadows. I dodged in between bits of metal debris, cast-offs from a previous age. I bumped into objects, cutting my dress and bruising my skin. Cranes rusted overhead and I ran over discarded chains. I tried not to kick anything that would make a noise and give my position away. It was a jungle of discarded machinery. Sharp objects bit into my skin, one shoe came off but I hadn't the time to stop and pick it up. Sharp objects cut into my feet, but I was so numb with cold and fear I could barely feel the pain. I tripped over some railway lines that were embedded into cobblestones. The brackish waters of the river smelled of seaweed, and in the far distance I heard the town hall clock striking two o'clock in the morning, the sound travelling over a sleepy town. I knew Granddad wouldn't be asleep, not as long as I was missing.

The ground beneath my feet suddenly felt different. I was no longer running on cobbles but wood. In the inky darkness and rain, I realised I had reached a jetty and had failed to find the dock gates.

Please, please help me someone!

Behind me my predator was coming closer. The realisation came to me that ahead there was no exit and that I was being pursued by a slayer of little girls. Dull moonlight reflected off the water, beneath which came the gentle swish of the tide hitting the bulwarks.

I desperately searched for a place to hide. Seeing four oil barrels, I rushed towards them. Rusting and empty they looked like the ramparts of a castle and a place to hide. Ducking down, I struggled to silence my gasping breath. On all fours, I felt the rotten wood of the jetty with my hands. In the distance, I could hear his voice, it was as cold as iron. "Ellie, where are you? You know you can't escape." He seemed to be enjoying the chase. "You've hurt me, which means I have to punish you and punish you I will. Understood?"

I felt my throat constrict as his threat carried through the rain. I crouched for a few minutes and hearing no sound, hoped I might get away with it. Hope drained away as Lassie, *her tail wagging, suddenly appeared on my side of the metal barrels. I gasped. My smell of fear had led her to me.*

One bark and it would be all over.

I fought off my panic. "Good girl." I whispered ever so softly in her ear, hugging and caressing her. I was her friend, no need to expose me. We both hated the same master, both of us wanted good to overcome evil. The dog gently licked my face. She knew. She was my friend, a good animal.

From the darkness the man's voice emerged. "Where are you, girl? Have you found something?"

The dog jerked her head and gave out a playful yelp. She thought it was a game and I let her go as she bolted away, towards her master.

"Good girl, you have found something, have you? Something behind those barrels I bet." His voice sounded close, his laugher like the cackle of a demented clown.

Gripped by fear I stood up and through the pelting rain I could see him, ten yards away. His dark figure was moving slowly towards me, through the curtain of rain, and even in dim light I was aware of his sinister smile. I turned and scampered into the darkness, running in the opposite direction, to get anywhere, as long as it was away from HIM.

Sprinting along the jetty, I recalled a French school lesson when we'd learned that 'jetée' in French means 'thrown'.

I could hear him laughing for he knew I was trapped, but I still ran into the dark unknown. Suddenly there was no more slippery wood beneath my feet. I was THROWN into the air as I ran off the edge, screaming as I fell.

My head hit a wooden crossbeam, knocking me out as I plunged into the river.

The water rushed up my nostrils, choking me. My mouth was clamped shut and my eyes opened as consciousness returned. The water was terribly cold and I struggled to hold my breath as little bubbles of air, like pearls escaping, floated past my face. My body panicked as I sank and my flailing was stronger than expected. The bottom of the river, thick with centuries-old, black, degraded flotsam and jetsam, engulfed me in a dirty black veil. I didn't want to fill my body with this corrupted mess; I knew I was going to drown and wanted clean water in my lungs. Kicking myself above the mix of murky mud, my eyes eventually peered through clear water. I felt at peace and didn't fight because I knew my time had come.

Why struggle?

I gasped and choked on the river water. It flowed into me slowly before it came with a rush; no panic, let it happen. Lungs filled, my used air escaped in large bubbles. Deep under water, I drifted under a wooden bulwark, part of the jetty, and became trapped.

That's the place where I died.

Eyes wide open, I watched later as crabs picked at the skin of my legs. Four hours later the tide turned and I floated away from my restraint and headed down river.

In the movies when a dead body is in the water, it's always face down. I suppose that's how most dead people float. But I was different; I was face up, eyes unblinking. The storm had passed. Perhaps I wanted to look at the starry night sky one more time. I bobbed like an empty bottle and gently floated headfirst. My arms stretched out and my long red hair drifted freely around my face.

I passed the empty shipyards, with their cranes and redundant winches watching me like a sad line of spectators. I slowly drifted past the disused coal wharves, where for a hundred years the coal from local pits had been brought by rail truck to be loaded onto ships bound for London. On the north side of the river the empty fish quay watched me go by. A former thriving market place, it was now as defunct as I was. On the south bank, the former Customs House, a magnificent Georgian stone building, now a theatre house slowly passed. I continued slowly, bobbing and drifting on the tide. I could hear the sound of a bell from a buoy, a ghostly toll marking my voyage down the river.

Gradually the groyne came into view, built to help the flow of the river and the place my mum said my daddy fished as a boy. I slowly passed its bell tower and was now in the harbour; the beams from the two lighthouses situated on the end of the piers, swept the night like searchlights.

A souther-easterly wind picked up and my body started to float towards some rocks known locally as the Black Middens. They had been a graveyard for ships under sail in the nineteenth century. Strong winds and poor seamanship had blown many a wooden ship onto the rocks. It's where my river trip ended, trapped on the rocks, under the watchful eye of Tynemouth Priory. Eventually a lonely starfish came along and kept me company.

Later, as the sun came up, an old man out looking for edible crabs found me. Within the hour I was in a police ambulance and speeding towards the mortuary table.

Chapter Seventeen

"We've found a body."

I gripped the phone in a stranglehold as my muscles stiffened up through my body. I then replaced the receiver.

In a daze, I pulled on my clothes, making time to collect a small pair of scissors from a kitchen drawer and an envelope from my office desk.

I was outside as the patrol car pulled up. The driver hardly had time to put his hand brake on and I was in the passenger seat. Despite it being early morning, he put on his siren and raced back to the station.

I went straight to Jill's office. She looked terrible, perhaps even older.

She said sombrely, "I'm so sorry, Tony. We found a girl's body this morning in the harbour. When you're ready, we need to go and see Arthur in the morgue."

I nodded that I was ready, well, as ready as I could be. I know about seeing bodies in the morgue. I've done it dozens of time. Before, it had been part of the job that was painful but went with the job description. I know about the agony families go through identifying a loved one. I know that I am a tired man. Not because I haven't slept, no, it's not that kind of tired. I'm tired because this is personal and there is nothing in the world that prepares you for it.

Jill looked into my eyes, hesitating. "I haven't informed Judy yet. We need formal identification; I guess you'll want to do that."

I nodded. "Best if I tell Judy myself. Best if it comes from me."

Arthur turned out to be a woman. She was Doctor Ann Arthur, a good-looking, middle-aged pathologist. A body lay on the slab, covered up with a white sheet. The walls of the morgue were just as I'd remembered: the white-washed brickwork was more a work place than a chapel of rest. Some of the equipment had been updated.

Doctor Arthur asked quietly, "Are you ready?"

I nodded, but it was a lie.

The doctor hesitated for a brief moment, then the sheet was gently pulled back and the room suddenly felt as if the air had been sucked out.

My Ellie lay there like a discarded mannequin. Was she at peace? I don't know. I knew I wasn't. The knots in my stomach nearly cut me in two; a sharp pain stabbed my brain. My hands were shaking and I made clenched fists to control the trembling.

Looking at the pathologist, I took my time to catch my breath before whispering, "It's her, that's our Ellie. Ellie Peach and," I muttered to myself, "twice as sweet."

Ellie's open eyes were like glass marbles staring at the ceiling. I gingerly stepped forward and, as if in a dream, gently closed her eyelids. I stroked her red hair and for a moment she looked alive, untouched and still my little girl, not a police crime statistic. I bent my head and softly placed a kiss on her forehead. I'd forgotten how a dead body feels; she was ice-cold to the touch because her essence has gone.

Where does it go when it's gone?

Fumbling in my jacket pocket and with shaking fingers, I removed the scissors and feeling I was bleeding inside, cut a lock of her beautiful hair. I sobbed, "I'm so sorry, Ellie, sorry Granddad let you down." Putting the strand into the envelope, I said to no one in particular, "For her mother." Then as an explanation, I added, "We all need the hair to remember our beautiful Ellie." I felt Jill's hand on my shoulder. I turned and informed her, "She's dressed differently. This dress she's wearing, it isn't hers, but looks similar to one she owns."

Jill removed her hand and inquired, "Are you telling me the clothes she's wearing are not the ones she had when she left home?"

My head slumped as I answered, "Yes, the dress she has on looks similar to the one she wore when she won her gold medal, but it's not what she wore when she left home."

Jill confirmed something that I already knew. "This means someone dressed her and that means she was definitely abducted." She headed for the door, "I'll inform Webster it's now an official murder enquiry."

On leaving I wandered the streets for an hour, walking around aimlessly. I was finding it difficult to breathe as if a hand was strangling my windpipe. A cold sweat covered my forehead and my fists were crunched into tight balls.

How do you tell a young mother her girl has been murdered? My daughter had already lost a husband, now her youngest child had gone.

I didn't need to say anything. My haggard look as I entered the house told her everything she needed to know. Judy howled like she's been slashed with a razor. Jack came into the room and he ran to his mother, wrapping his arms around her.

I breathed in slowly. It was like a thunderstorm was going off in my head. I could feel my daughter's grief and despair all bound together. I wanted to untie it, cast it out, but knew I couldn't. What she was feeling was a mirror image of my feelings, a wretchedness that was consuming us like a plague.

Judy disentangled herself from Jack. Kissing him gently on the cheek she came over to me. I put my arms out and we hugged. I could feel her heart beating in her chest like a frightened bird as my tears mingled with hers. Jack sobbed behind her.

I eventually said despondently, "I'll put the kettle on."

Two cups of tea later and Judy had no more tears left. I decided not to hide the truth from them. I informed them it was murder.

Judy didn't say a thing; I think she already knew. Jack looked at me with grief and anger in his eyes; it was at this point it became personal for him. He said in a dry voice as he reached out and grabbed my arm, "We'll get the bastard, won't we Granddad?"

I nodded my head, "Yes Jack, we'll get him all right."

Six hours later I was back in Jill's office.

She waved some papers in her hand, "I've got the autopsy report. Do you want to read it?"

I shook my head, "Just give me the headlines."

Jill paused, gathering her thoughts, she then started: "Ellie had been in the water six to eight hours. Time of death was between midnight and three o'clock and cause of death was by drowning." She looked at me sadly, "If it's possible, there is some good news, Tony." She paused again and then stated, "Ellie hadn't been molested."

I blurted out, "Are you sure?"

"Absolutely. Doctor Arthur is adamant, no rape or any sort of interference took place, but it seems Ellie hadn't eaten for a while. Her stomach was completely empty and the Doc thinks she might have been starved for a few days." She paused whilst I processed the information. "There were cuts and blisters on her finger tips, which remain a mystery, plus some other cuts and bruising on her body that you would expect having been in a river. There was a bruise on her forehead, which may have been the result of a fall or a blow from a blunt instrument." She paused again looking around the room, only this time she was perturbed. She finally looked at me and said, "Tony, she was without under garments, no knickers."

I asked, "So what have we got?"

Jill blinked and answered, "Possible scenario: the killer struck her about the head and threw her unconscious body into the river."

I said thoughtfully, "Strange she wasn't molested and strange someone took the trouble to dress her up in the skating dress. That suggests someone who is calculating."

I spoke slowly, gathering my thoughts as the words came out. "I think the dress suggests some sort of symbolism, perhaps a ritual. The starving might have been a power thing or he was trying to get the victim to submit, again a power lust. I think the lack of under clothes suggest the main motivation was sexual, but he never got to satisfy his goal." I raised my eyes. "I think Ellie escaped and she died whilst trying to get away."

Jill said with mild admiration, "Webster did tell me you were good. What now?"

"I think you need to bring in Jimmy Temple for an interview."

****

I watched through a two-way mirror as on the other side Jill and DC Sweetman started their interview with Ellie's skating coach, Jimmy Temple.

DS Jill Adams started, "How long have you known Ellie Peach?"

Temple looked uneasy and adjusted himself on his chair. "About five years, I was her skating coach. She had real talent, did Ellie." Almost as an afterthought, he added, "I saw her once a week for an hour. Her mother was always with her and if not, her grumpy granddad turned up."

Jill glanced up to the mirror as Sweetman asked, "Where were you on the afternoon of the sixteenth Mr Temple?"

"I was driving to my caravan. I have a holiday caravan near Marsden Bay. Why am I being interviewed?"

"We're interviewing everyone with a connection to the victim," Sweetman wrote in his notebook then asked, "Can anyone verify your story?"

Jimmy's eyes narrowed, "I played Scrabble with a neighbour, he'll collaborate I was at my caravan."

"What time was this?"

Jimmy looked momentarily confused. "Not sure. I would guess, about seven-thirty at night."

"What about between two o'clock and four on the same day?"

"I told you, I was driving to the caravan."

"What sort of car do you have?"

"It's a Ford Escort."

"Colour?"

"White with lots of rust," Jimmy had a slight impediment and lisped his words.

Jill asked, "Is that a car or a van?"

"Van," replied Jimmy. He then added, "It's taxed and has an up-to-date MOT."

"You live on the north side, near Whitley Bay?"

"Yes." Jimmy frowned.

"Why do you have you a caravan south of the river? Isn't Whitley Bay a holiday spot?"

"It's not a crime to have a holiday home at Marsden. Besides, what's the point of having a holiday home in your own backyard?" Jimmy folded his arms across his chest.

"You do know Marsden is only a few miles from Ellie's home?"

Jimmy lowered his voice. "I knew she lived on the south side, but I've never been to her house, I swear."

"Where were you last night?"

Jimmy nearly exploded, "This is ridiculous. I had nothing to do with Ellie's death." He paused as he calmed down a little. Rubbing his hands he said, "Told you already. I was at my caravan. I'm due to go home today."

"Can anyone substantiate your story?"

"Not sure, I stayed in all last night and watched TV."

Sweetman gave a tight smile. "I don't think you'll be going home today, Jimmy."

Jill concluded, "Mr Temple, I have to advise you I'm not satisfied with your story, and we'll be holding you over night whilst we continue our investigations. I suggest you get yourself a good lawyer."

Next day, the local paper ran the headline: '*Skating coach held over girl's brutal murder.*'

I hate journalists; they are real vultures feeding off the carcasses of people's misfortune. Jimmy's name made it into the papers but the bottom line was, despite him being the owner of a white van, there was no evidence to connect him to Ellie's death. Jimmy's lawyer got him released two days later, although he remained a person of interest to the investigation. My nonce radar didn't seem to be switched on. I couldn't make up my mind if he was a slime ball or not.

Four days later the funeral took place. Jimmy phoned the day before and asked if he could attend. I lied and said it was family only. Lots of other people turned up, including press photographers, and in a sad, lonely cemetery we laid Ellie's body to rest in the ground. Dark clouds crept over the treetops threatening rain. Ellie's headstone was already in place although the letters hadn't yet been chiselled onto it. It was something I wanted to do and I had arranged with the undertaker to make an exception and have the stone in place for the funeral. He agreed to finish off the lettering at a later date. I didn't want my beloved granddaughter put into a hole in the ground like unwanted rubbish. I needed her place marked so she would know we cared.

I was surprised that Jill wasn't there as she said she would attend. After the coffin had been laid to rest at the bottom of a freshly dug hole, the family and other mourners slowly made their way to the cars. A cloud of despondency followed us, misery in every footstep. Some of Ellie's school friends continued weeping.

I saw a flustered Jill threading through the obelisks and tombs. A moss-covered, stone angel watched her as she approached us. She looked dressed for a funeral and was obviously looking for me. She nodded her condolences to Judy as she came up to my shoulder.

"Tony," she took my arm and led me away from the others. She was puffed from walking so fast and her face looked flushed. She announced urgently, "Tony, we've found another body."

Jill updated me as we drove to the police mortuary. "She was found this morning, floating in the river. We think her name is Mary Jackson. She was reported missing last night from a local children's care home. But because she's absconded before, the staff didn't report the fact to the police until two this morning."

I asked, "How old was she?"

"Twelve, the same age as Ellie," Jill made a pained face.

"What was she wearing when her body was found?"

"She was naked, Tony."

Doctor Arthur showed us into her chilly theatre of work. She spoke matter of fact. "I've done a preliminary autopsy." She paused, then announced,

"This one was raped both vaginally and I'm afraid, anally."

Looking at the body my breath stopped dead in my chest. I could see the cadaver was covered in bruises; the rape had been vicious. A front tooth was broken. I asked, "Are these bruises a direct result of the attack?"

The good doctor replied, "Yes, it was a very brutal assault. She suffered a broken eye socket."

"Did she die in the water?" After the funeral, I thought I had no grief left, but my conscience managed to prick some reserve and it came in the form of weariness.

The doctor shook her head. "No she was killed first, strangulation then dumped into the river."

My hands were sweating, "Any family?" I scratched my eyebrow.

Jill interjected, "I'm afraid there was a reason why she was in a children's home. There was no one but the care assistants and the State."

I retorted, "And they let her down." There was a long pause, perhaps we were respecting the dead, but eventually Jill asked, "Anything else, Doctor?"

"Yes I'm afraid there is. Inside her vagina I found a rolled up photo." She looked at me sadly, "It's a photograph of your Ellie, skating on the ice."

I put my fingers behind my shirt collar and tugged at my tie, which was tight and felt in danger of choking me. The tie was a reminder I had just attended a funeral. My skull felt it was being attacked by thousands of agonising six-inch nails.

Jill turned to me and whispered, "What do you think, Tony?"

My voice sounded grave as I announced, "There seems to be a lot of anger in this attack. It's the same person and this time he was frustrated and boiling over with rage. I think the tipping point, the cause of the fury, was the fact Ellie did get away, so her abductor quickly looked for another victim." I swallowed hard as I gathered my thoughts, fighting the feeling of nausea. "I think the photo is some sort of message."

Chapter Eighteen

*H*eaven only knows where I was and then I thought, Ellie, silly girl, THIS is heaven!

An overpowering feeling of intense unconditional love flowed through my body, making me glow all over. Smiling I walked with a feeling of floating, by a river of such brilliance and colours I could not begin to describe them. I saw a majestic waterfall, where the Technicolor water cascaded and fell in complete silence. On the riverbank trees and flowers exploded into bloom as I passed them, their scent delighting my nose. Transparent shimmering butterflies floated by in this idyllic landscape and the sky was streaked with blue and gold. I continued my odyssey filled with wonder at the melody of sights that pleased my eye, making my soul swell with joy. Eventually, I came to a beach and watched more butterflies floating and fluttering around the dunes. Feeling at peace, I saw the sea was a deep blue, bluer than any sea I'd ever seen before, and in the surf red and white striped dolphins were playing with a beach ball. Above my head, multi-coloured seagulls soared in silence. There was no wind and I could hear music and recognised the music of a carousel. Walking towards the sound, each step felt like an explosion of colour, love and beauty as the warm sand tickled between my toes.

Soon I came upon the merry-go-round and it was the most magnificent one I'd ever seen. The colours on the galloping wooden horses, dragons, zebras and tigers were really bright and thousands of fairy lights flashed in time with the music. It was the coolest fairground ride I'd ever seen and on a flying horse, holding onto the barley-twist pole with one hand sat a girl. She waved madly to me with her free arm.

Her voice carried over the music. "Hello, Ellie. I've been expecting you."

"My name's Jessica." The pretty girl had bright blue eyes and looked about two years older than me. She dismounted the ride and walked over to me. She asked, "Have you seen the film, Mary Poppins?"

I nodded and noticed the music as well as the ride had stopped. I replied, "A long time ago." Granddad had bought me the video for a Christmas present a few years ago.

"Isn't it just the BEST film, EVER! This merry-go-round is exactly like the one in the movie. Some days the wooden animals actually fly, just as in the movie. Isn't it wonderful?"

I looked at the girl with amazement. "Awesome. The rides can actually fly?"

Yes," Jessica nodded her head enthusiastically.

"Is that because this is heaven?"

Jessica confirmed with a smile, "Yes, this is heaven."

"Are we the only ones here?"

"No, silly, heaven is full, but everyone gets to build their own version. This is mine. Welcome!"

I hesitated, "So are you my guardian angel?"

She touched my shoulder with a very gentle hand. "No, more like, now what do they call it? I know, I'm a soul mate."

I frowned. "What's that?"

Jessica withdrew her hand and paused. "A soul mate is like a heavenly mentor."

Shaking my head, I retorted, "I don't know what a mentor is."

"Oh, a mentor is a kind of pal who shows you how things work, shows you the ropes."

"Like my granddad."

"Yes, I suppose he's a type of mentor."

"So if this is heaven, does that mean God really exists?"

Jessica laughed. "Nobody knows. He's as big a mystery here as He was before. There are no answers, just happiness."

"So how do I build my heaven?"

She smiled. "It's already done, it's behind you."

Turning around I saw a large dull building, which I hadn't seen before. It was rotund, with a low-domed roof and no windows. Despondent and disappointed, I burst out, "That's my heaven?"

"Yes," said Jessica with a jolly voice. It's where you'll be happiest." She concluded with a grin, "It must mean something to you."

I felt miserable and my words were hardly audible. "It looks like a giant pork pie."

Jessica's grin faded and she shrugged nonchalantly, "Do you like pies? Perhaps the building's full of nice pastries? Yummy."

"I hate pies, hate them. This can't be right. There has to be some mistake."

"No such things as mistakes in heaven. What I can tell you is the door is locked and even you can't get in."

"What?"

"No keys. If the building, your heaven, is locked down it can only mean one thing."

"What's that?"

Jessica raised an eyebrow. "Heaven's not quite ready for you. You have to go back."

"Back where?"

"Back where you've just come from, silly, to the other side."

I stepped back, my hands falling by my side. "What! Like a ghost?"

"Don't be silly, ghosts don't exist."

"So will I be visible to people?"

She shrugged. "Sometimes, people may see you just before they die; otherwise, you'll be invisible to all."

Bewildered, I asked, "So why do I have to go back?"

She paused and looked at me. "You have to go back and try to stop two murders."

I gasped and brought my hand to my lips. "Murders! Who's going to be killed?"

Jessica shrugged. "Well, there's a poor girl called Mary, but you won't be able to stop her death."

I looked at my new friend in amazement. "So who else is going to be murdered?"

She answered grimly, "Your gran' daddy and brother Jack."

The carousel music started up again, but when I lifted my eyes towards it, I saw that it was different and when I looked back at Jessica, she was gone. I recognised the ride; this merry-go-round was the one from my home town, the one at the beach fair.

I had gone back.

The fair was crowded and I quickly realised nobody could see me. I was invisible. Awesome!

People walked by, nobody gave me a second look, a mischievous thought occurred to me I should go inside the ghost train and REALLY have some fun, then I saw her.

There was an aura of sadness about her. She looked about my age, but her cheap dress and shabby coat were secondhand; even the smile on her face looked recycled. I felt my skin shiver all over and I didn't know the reason why. I followed her and watched as she bought a bag of chips. She counted out the pennies and seemed relieved to have enough money. She ate the chips like a starved person, throwing on lots of vinegar to cool down the fried food so she could stuff them quickly into her mouth. I watched her as she searched for a bin to deposit her rubbish. She visited the public toilets, had a pee and washed her hands, removing any grease from around her lips. Afterwards, she stood at the waltzer and mouthed the words of the pop music being played through the speakers. Two teenage boys came up to her and talked. Eventually, they got bored and left. She looked abandoned.

I had no idea why I felt compelled to follow her. With the sun setting, she started walking towards the exit, passing stallholders as they finished for the day.

Outside, she crossed the road and skirted around the park that faced the fair. I continued following her, like a soldier on a mission, with enthusiasm but no understanding of the reason. I wondered if my dad always knew the reasons for his military orders, or did he just obey without question?

We were walking up a tree-lined avenue, going uphill with the park on our right when I saw it.

It was the white van.

It was parked at the kerb and the passenger window was down. As the girl drew alongside I heard his voice.

"Excuse me young lady, could you possibly help me?"

I wanted to shout to her to get away, but I seemed paralysed, frozen to the spot.

I heard her voice, which was still that of a young girl, sweet and innocent. She stopped and bending her head looked into the van. "What is it?"

Still unable to move, I heard the monster say, "See my lovely dog in the back, she's so sad because she's lost her little puppy. You haven't seen it, have you?"

The girl shook her head.

"What's your name darling?"

"Mary."

"Mary, can you be kind and help me find the puppy? I bet he's really scared."

The girl nodded her head. "I suppose so."

The passenger door swung open and a hand went out and helped Mary get in. The van pulled away and she was gone.

I watched as he dragged poor Mary her into the warehouse. Ignoring her screams, he ripped her clothes off and had his evil way with her. The dog was left in the van, so was saved from watching the horror, but I wasn't so lucky. I watched with open mouth. Satisfaction for the monster didn't come quickly.

Like an animal he tore into her flesh before turning the poor girl over and violating her in a heinous manner. I screamed he should stop, but of course my words were locked in another place, another world. With saliva frothing at his lips, he strangled her.

I watched with pity as he carried her broken, naked body to the jetty and heard the splash as she was dumped into the river. I felt impotent, unable to help, but as the creature drove away, I swore on my daddy's grave, this would be the last child he would murder. I then went into a corner of the warehouse and sobbed, howling until there were no more tears left.

Granddad never got on with Jimmy. Gramps even told my coach to stay away from my funeral, but it was unnecessary. By the time they laid my body into the cold ground Jimmy was dead.

Chapter Nineteen

I was still at the police station in an open-necked shirt, the funeral tie in my jacket pocket, when the call came in. Jill looked as white as a ghost when she shot me a tight look. "Tony, we've found another body."

We drove to Marsden Bay and walked down the many wooden steps to the beach. The cliffs were over three hundred feet in height and the local press would call it a "popular" place to commit suicide., It was true, over the years a few people had jumped over the edge, but to call it that seemed inappropriate. Jimmy's corpse was hidden behind some rocks, which is why the early morning dog walkers had not stumbled upon it. It took two young lads playing pirates to scramble over the rocks and find his broken body.

Jill muttered, "Looks like he jumped. His head's opened up like a broken egg."

I didn't say anything, just nodded and acknowledged Dr Arthur who was standing next to a crime scene police photographer.

Jimmy's caravan was a ten-minute walk from the cliff and when Jill and I arrived the two of us were surprised to see Webster. There was a triumphant grin on his face.

"We've got a result, looks like our Jimmy was a two-time murderer, slime ball." Webster could hardly contain his glee.

Jill looked exasperated; head to one side, her face blanched. "Sir, what are you doing here?"

Webster gave a natural shrug and as an explanation said, "The big boss upstairs went ballistic this morning with the news of a second dead child. Only bloody used the 'F word' down the telephone! Can you believe it? Told me to get my arse in gear and tidy up the mess, then loser Jimmy does the noble thing, executes himself and leaves a confession."

I barked, "A confession?"

"Yes, also in the caravan is tons of evidence to tie this miserable son of a bitch to the deaths. Sorry, Tony, I know one of the victims was your granddaughter, but good news, eh? We've got a result."

The three of us stood inside Jimmy's caravan. Outside, blue and white police tape surrounded the vehicle and a young constable stood guard. Almost tidy, the place was a bachelor's bolthole. A mobile of Disney characters hung from the ceiling. Dirty dishes stood in the sink, and a half drunk bottle of beer plus a packet of strong cigarettes lay on the table.

Webster announced, "Look here." He indicated a Scrabble board spread out on the table. On the game board, spread out in letter tiles was written: 'SORRY I KILLED THE TWO KIDS CANT LIVE WITH MYSELF'.

I looked at Webster and asked incredulously, "That's the confession?"

He waved his hand like he was swatting a fly. "Oh, I know what you're thinking: it's all bullshit, not his handwriting, wouldn't stand up in court, but what about these?" With a smug look, he held up three plastic evidence bags, I could see two wristwatches and a photo. "Recognise the watch, Tony?"

I let out a long, quiet breath. "It looks like Ellie's. The one I gave to her for her birthday."

"BINGO! And I bet my police pension this one belongs to the other girl and guess what? The photo is of Ellie and it's exactly like the one we found stuffed up the second victim. Bloody trophies; the sick bastard, we found all these hidden in the caravan."

I asked for the evidence bags and looked at the watch. No doubt, it was the one I'd bought for Ellie. The photo showed Ellie in the middle of an ice skating sequence. She was wearing the dress her mum had bought specially for her last competition. She had a broad smile and I resisted a tear that tried to escape, rubbing my nose with the back of my hand.

Jill retorted, "It's all a bit neat, isn't sir?" She was angry Webster had turned up and walked all over her crime scene and investigation.

He replied, "Listen love, I won't insult your intelligence by saying it is absolutely watertight, but the fact is, confession can be good for the soul and what we've got here is a confession." He paused, then in his 'superior officer' voice said, "Unless you disagree, DS Adams."

Jill knew this was a battle she couldn't win, so she said, "No, sir."

Webster did his market stallholder pitch. "Listen love, you're still the principle investigation officer, think how good it'll look on your CV; a double murder result."

Looking crestfallen, Jill remained silent.

The caravan door swung open and DC Sweetman's head appeared. He sounded animated, "Sir, we think we've found a warehouse by the river where the little girls may have been held."

About a dozen uniformed officers were searching the warehouse when we arrived. It was situated in a small boat repair yard. The yard and warehouse looked as if they had been abandoned for years.

Inside stood a set of gym weights with bench and nearby was a wooden shed, possibly a storage place for tools. Two of the officers were looking into an open-top Texaco oil drum. The space was filled with the smell of smoke and misery.

One of the officers shouted over to Sweetman, "Looks like someone's tried to have a bonfire, sir."

Jill and her colleague walked over whilst I headed for the shed. If Ellie had been captive here for days, the shed would make an ideal cell. On the door and external frame, I saw four U-shaped metal hooks secured into the door and woodwork, ideal for slotting the wooden bar leaning against the doorframe. You only need this sort of security to keep someone prisoner.

Inside I could hardly breathe. There was an old wooden chair and a mattress on the floor. In the corner stood an old military type of jerrycan. I lifted it. It felt almost full, about five gallons. Picking up the chair I could see its four leg prints in the dust. The jerrycan had no such footprints suggesting it had recently been deposited in the hut. I screwed the cap off and smelled the contents. It was petrol. Putting the cap back on, I looked around; my instinct was telling me this WAS the place where poor Ellie had been held as she waited for me to rescue her. The place where all her hope had drained away.

My head dropped and I heard myself say, "I'm so sorry, sweet pea."

Ignoring the wretchedness that flowed through my body, I kneeled down and lifted the corner of the rough bed. Seeing some sort of object, I put my hand into the dark and brought out three squashed drink cans. Looking at the ensemble I realised this was a deliberate piece of engineering; this had been built for a purpose. It was too big to unpick locks, too soft to lever anything. And then I saw what could be a trace of dried blood.

A dagger!

A thin smile passed my lips. "Well done, Ellie." I placed the instrument carefully into an evidence bag. A shadow fell across the floor and I turned.

Jill was at the shed door. "Tony, you need to see this."

In the hall of the warehouse, the contents of the drum were scattered on the floor and a forensic guy was shifting through the partly burnt remains. I could see the majority of the stuff was clothes, girls' stuff. I recognised a partially burnt shoe belonging to Ellie. A large blob of melted black plastic lay to the side.

DC Sweetman kneeled down and inspected the plastic mess. After a few minutes of reflection he announced, "Sir, I think I know what this is."

Webster walked around to his side, looking like a kid on a treasure hunt. "Tell me, Sherlock. It's a load of melted plastic, what the fuck do you think it was?"

Sweetman ignored the boorishness and said with enthusiasm, "Sir, there's something caught in the plastic, I think I recognise what it is."

"Well son, don't keep your superintendent in suspense, what the fuck is it?"

"I think it's a voice changer. My nephew has one; I bought it for him last Xmas."

"Well?" Webster sounded impatient.

The young DC declared, "It's part of a Darth Vader costume mask."

Webster boomed out, "Darth Vader, you fucking with me, Sweetie? If you are I'll give your balls to your boss to wear as earrings."

Jill butted in, "Thanks for the thought, boss, nice gift to give a girly, earrings." Her sarcasm was lost on Webster. "But I think the DC may have something. A helmet mask and voice changer would hide the killer's identity."

Webster sounded as if he had swallowed a fishbone. He bluffed, "Of course it would, I knew that straight away, sorry about the earrings, love. Don't want to sound like a chauvinist pig."

Jill lied, "No offence taken, sir."

The forensic officer, now on all fours, announced, "I have something here of interest." Using a small pair of tweezers he extracted from the debris a partially burnt piece of paper. Bringing it to his face he declared, "A gas bill, the name is still intact, it's," bringing the paper even closer to his face, he said, "a J. Temple."

Webster nearly jumped up and down. "Bingo! Fucking full house, we have the bastard now." He turned to Jill and said with neanderthal zeal, "Well done, DS Adams, bloody well done, bonny lass."

I exclaimed, "I don't think…"

Webster cut me short. "I don't give a rat's arse what you think, Tony." He licked his lips. "The file is now officially closed and you're off the case." He spat out, "Thank you for all your help."

I glared at him, not believing what I was hearing.

Jill spluttered, "But…"

Webster growled as he interrupted his subordinate, "No 'buts'! The case has been solved."

Anger twisted my heart as I watched Webster swagger away. As he approached the door, I saw the heel of his right shoe sink into something soft on the floor. Outside he jumped into his car and drove away with a triumphant squeal of tyres, no doubt on his way to report the good news to his superior.

A few minutes later I sat in Jill's car.

She asked, "Where can I take you, Tony?"

I rubbed the top of my thigh with my hand and dampened down the internal rage. I noticed my hands were clamped shut, my tendons too tight to straighten my fingers. I replied bitterly, "I guess I should go home and get out of these clothes."

Jill switched on the engine letting it idle for a few minutes. She murmured with an apologetic voice, "Sorry about Webster. I'll miss working with you."

"I think he enjoyed firing me. Some twelve year-old itch he's finally scratched."

"Webster's an arsehole."

I replied, "Nothing new then."

Her eyes softened. "Do you think Jimmy Temple is our man?"

I handed her the evidence bag with the Coke cans. "Check out the blood on this with the pathologist, I bet it isn't Jimmy's. Also ask Dr Arthur if there's a stab wound on his body."

"Tony, Webster's going to close the file, just to keep his superiors happy. Are you suggesting we haven't caught our man?"

"Don't you think it all looks a little contrived…?"

"I'm not sure what to think, Tony."

I snapped, "It's a farce, the evidence was meant to be found. Someone has laid down a false trail, and Webster's running around like a bloodhound with two tails following the wrong scent."

"So who are we looking for?"

I replied earnestly, "A crazy man with a stab wound, a white van and a dog."

She looked surprised. "A dog?"

"Yes, he has a dog, probably uses it to lure the kids."

"How do you know this?"

"Because at this moment, an angry Webster is in his car, wiping dog shit from his shoe."

Jill smiled. "I need something more than dog shit for an arsehole to change its mind."

A long silence followed before I said, "Jimmy couldn't have taken the photos."

"Why not?" Jill's forehead corrugated as she frowned.

I replied, "The photographs are of Ellie at her last skating competition, just a few weeks ago."

Jill spun her head towards me. "How are you sure?"

"It's the only time she ever wore that dress."

"Wasn't Jimmy there?"

"Yes he was."

"So how come he couldn't have taken the kiddie snaps?"

"If you look at the angle of the shot, someone was looking down when they pressed the shutter."

"And Jimmy?"

"Jimmy was at floor level during the whole time Ellie was skating. I know that for a fact. He couldn't have taken the photo."

"So whoever took the photo was amongst the spectators."

"That's correct."

"So our abductor was in the audience when she won the competition. It would go towards explaining the look-a-like dress, I suppose. But to be honest, Tony, I think Webster's got his mind fixed on this." She said tentatively, "It'll take more than a photo angle to change his mind."

"I know."

She said apologetically, "Sorry, Tony, I really am. I'll give it my best shot, but don't hold out for anything."

I turned my head, I said sadly. "Don't take me home, Jill. Drive me to Judy's. At least my daughter will need her dad."

As Jill put the car into gear, the transmission made a crunching sound and for a brief moment I thought the reverberation was from deep inside my heart.

Chapter Twenty

*A*fter I watched the monster dump Mary's body I followed him to a caravan park. When I say, I followed him what really happened was I watched as his white van drove away from the dock, then I'm watching him arrive at his destination. I don't physically follow I just turn up. I guess that's how things work when you come back from the other side.

I recognised the area; I could see the lighthouse in the far distance to my left and guessed we were near a place called Marsden. It was a quarter after midnight and the caravan park was in darkness. As it was low season, most were empty and only one had its lights on. The monster pulled out of his anorak pocket a supermarket plastic carry bag, the heavy-duty type. There were quite a few rocks on the ground and he selected one, about the size of a lawn bowling ball. Feeling its heaviness he put the rock into the bag. The plastic straps strained under the weight.

I watched as he went to the caravan with the lights on. He walked up the three steps and he knocked on the door.

When eventually the door opened I gasped. Jimmy my coach was standing there.

"What the bloody hell do you want at this time of night?" Jimmy sounded slightly drunk.

I shouted, "Run." But of course, my voice didn't carry; it was trapped in another dimension, on the other side of a thick window in some other universe and I could only watch with mounting despair.

The monster had his back to me. "Sorry to wake you up, mate, but I've lost my dog; you haven't seen a collie have you? She's run off, never done anything like that before."

"Sorry pal, I've been in all night, best of luck, but I can't help you."

The monster turned, walked a few paces and said, "Couldn't help me could you? Two of us looking will be easier."

"No way, I'm turning in."

The monster turned his head. He said angrily, "What! You don't give a fuck about a missing dog?" He turned and with a softer tone called, "Hello girl, where are you?"

Jimmy replied, "I'll ignore your remark. Now if you don't get off the park I'll tell the police that you're trespassing."

The monster ignored Jimmy's threat and dropping to his knees looked under the caravan. He raged, "You bastard, my dog is here! You've killed it."

"What?" A shocked Jimmy ran down the steps as the monster stood up. Before any more words were said Jimmy dropped on all fours to see for himself if he did indeed have a dead dog under his mobile home. There wasn't one, of course.

The next action happened so quickly.

The monster dropped the stone out of the plastic bag and before it hit the ground had the bag tight over Jimmy's head. Jimmy struggled but the monster was on his back trapping him. Then the monster picked up the stone and crushed poor Jimmy's skull. Blood and brains splattered inside the bag. The monster was leaving no forensic evidence. Keeping the bag on his victim's head, the monster carried the body to the cliff. Taking off the bag he threw Jimmy's body into the night air. As the body crashed onto the rocks below, the sound of breaking bones startled some gulls off their nests.

Back at the caravan and wearing gloves, the monster hid two watches under the mattress. I noticed one of the watches was my birthday gift from Granddad. He hid a photograph under some socks in a drawer before searching amongst Jimmy's papers until one brought a smile to his lips. He put it inside his pocket. The last thing he did before leaving was arrange some letters on the Scrabble board. Whilst he did this, he hummed a well-known Beach Boys' song.

Back at the warehouse, the monster put the blood-splattered plastic bag and the Darth Vader mask into a tall, open-top oil drum. He produced a jerrycan of petrol and splashed some into the rusty container. After storing the jerrycan in the wooden shed, he returned and dropped a burning match into the drum. Black acrid smoke escaped as the monster started adding clothes to the fire. I recognised some as my own. Soon a fire blazed away reflecting yellow lights around the building. Before the incineration completed its work, the monster placed a metal top on the bin, starving the flames of oxygen and putting them out. The lid was discarded and taking the document he stole from Jimmy's caravan, his killer took another match and partially burnt the paper, carefully blowing it out before it was completely destroyed. He dropped the remains into the drum. I still couldn't see his face, but I was aware of his evil, clever smile, which indicated satisfaction at a job well done.

★★★★

I watched Granddad come into the kitchen. It was early morning, the day of my funeral. Jack was already up. He made Mum a cup of tea and took it to her in bed. Granddad had stayed overnight and neither of them looked as if they had got any sleep.

"How are you, Jack?"

My brother gave a thin smile. Sitting at the table with a bowl of cereals, he wasn't eating, only moving the food around the dish with a spoon. "I'm okay Granddad, although it feels like I've taken a bullet to the heart. Despite that, I guess I'm coping. I've never been to a funeral before."

With a sad voice, Granddad replied, "I know it's painful, we're all hurting, son. I've been to too many funerals, although I have to say, nothing prepares you for this. Jack you're going to have to be brave today. Not just for Ellie but for your mum. She needs a strong man to hold on to. It's got to be you Jack. Are you up for it, lad?"

"Of course," Jack shrugged and gave another thin smile.

"And I'll be here for you, son. That's how families get through this sort of thing. Ellie wouldn't want us to be too sad; she would want us to celebrate her life. Remember the good times, Jack, the good times."

157

"I spoilt the good times, didn't I?" My brother threw his spoon onto the table and, standing up, pushed back his chair with his legs. A veil of despair covered him.

Granddad walked over and held him by the shoulders. Looking deep into my brother's eyes, he said, "This is not the time for regrets, Jack. It's just that fate stole from you the opportunity to show Ellie how good a brother you could be. Your sister will know this, where ever she is."

My brother looked on the brink of tears. "Do you think she's looking down?"

"I'm sure, Jack, she'll be looking down and smiling. Remember Ellie loved you, loved us all, very much and that love was unconditional, do you understand?"

Jack nodded in a melancholy way. "I understand, Granddad."

I looked across the room at the two men I loved and smiled. How I wish they could see how wide my smile was.

Mum came down and walked into the kitchen. She whispered to my brother, "Thanks for the tea, Jack." She was a war widow veteran, so I thought perhaps she had already developed a coping strategy for death of a loved one. She continued, "I took Ellie's ice skates to the undertaker. She's being buried in her dress, the one she wore when she won gold. She's also wearing the skates. I just wish she had the medal."

Granddad put his arms around Mum, "Don't worry, Judy. I've had a copy made. I took it to the undertakers late last night. Had to knock them up, but they do advertise a twenty-four-hour service."

"Oh, Dad, thank you." Tears welled up, but the fountainhead was dry. "It gives me such comfort, my little girl, being..." She couldn't finish her words.

"What time do the cars arrive?" I think Jack knew the answer, he just wanted to keep Mum's mind away from the grief.

"Eleven o'clock," answered my mother.

I cried out, "I love you all." But of course they couldn't hear me. Had I thought about it, the fact they couldn't hear me could have saddened me, but I was determined not to be sad at my own funeral.

At eleven o'clock prompt my coffin and the cars arrived. The black hearse was a Bentley as were the following two cars. Jack, Mum and Granddad sat in the first, while Dad's sister and my cousins rode in the second. Four other cars followed in a convoy for the short journey.

Granddad brought a tube of boiled mints out of his pocket. "Suck these, they'll help." He gave Jack and Mum a sweet each before popping one into his own mouth.

After a twenty-minute journey, we drove up the leafy avenue towards the cemetery and I could see crowds of sad people waiting at the gates. A few press photographers were taking pictures. It felt as if I was some sort of princess or pop star, not some sad murder victim.

A short service was held at the chapel and my body was carried out to my grave. Mr Haines and a pupil from my school joined Granddad and Jack as pall-bearers. I smiled when I saw it was Adam and my grin turned to joy when a tear fell down his cheek. Fellow pupils including Talia were sobbing. *Mum remained strong until the ropes went under the oak box and I was lowered into the ground, when she broke down with a wail that echoed around the cemetery. My aunt brought a basket of petals and each person took a handful and scattered them on my coffin, as a final gesture, a last goodbye. Flowers were laid and school friends placed teddy bears on my headstone.*

As my family walked away, the gravediggers started shovelling the soil and clay into my resting place. 'Dust to dust'.

I saw my granddad's lady police friend manoeuvring herself through the crowd. She looked as if she had a message and I already knew what it was. They'd found poor Mary.

Chapter Twenty-One

Nature hates a vacuum and the loss of Ellie created a black hole in our universe. Judy became morose and tried to act as normal as she could for Jack's sake, but she couldn't hide the weight loss. Jack initially internalised his misery, but realised to turn inwards would only take him back to a place he'd inhabited before Ellie's murder. He seemed a different boy, one who could discuss his feelings and would actively listen if anyone talked to him. I just wished he'd changed twelve months earlier.

I shared with the two of them my theory that Jimmy wasn't the killer and the thought kept Jack's head above the waterline. I wouldn't be surprised if he spent the majority of his time fantasising what he would do when he caught his sister's predator.

Meanwhile, I was like road kill, stiff and crushed. Worms of misery ate at my carcass. Of course I never let it show to my daughter or my grandson; with them

I acted the responsible adult. I should have been awarded an Oscar for my performance. At night I would call the Samaritans and ask for Jenny, who would listen for an hour if she was on duty. That and the whisky helped a little.

A week later I found myself sitting with Jill in the County Hotel. She'd just come off duty and nursed a half pint of beer that sat on a table in front of her. It was raining and dark outside.

She reached over and touched my hand. "How are you doing, Tony?"

The truth was I was feeling chilled to the bone. It was as if my internal thermostat had switched itself off. I couldn't imagine ever feeling warm again. I told a half truth. "Getting through, I guess."

Sitting back in her chair, her elbow on the chair rest, she brought her hand under her chin and asked, "How about Judy and Jack?"

"They don't know it, but I guess time will help, although I guess the pain will never entirely go away."

Jill saw the tired and disappointed look on my pale face. She asked wistfully, "You saw the press report, then?"

I replied with more bitterness than I should have. I gave a sarcastic sigh, "The one telling the world, the case is closed on the two deaths and the police are no longer looking for anybody in connection with the abductions?"

Jill shook her head. "You shouldn't believe everything you read in the papers, Tony."

I squinted at her and muttered through my teeth, "I believed that report because you were the one giving the interview."

"It's only partially true," Jill said flatly.

"How can something be partially true? There is only truth or otherwise, nothing in between."

"You sound like a Baptist preacher."

I gave a tired sigh. "Okay, tell me the bits in between." I brought my glass to my lips and drank a large mouthful of beer.

Jill waited until I brought my glass back to the table before starting. "It's true we've got no more resources on the case, but the file remains open, hoping for more evidence to come in. Which means if anything does appear, I can have time and resources to investigate it officially."

I looked at her in astonishment. "Bloody hell. How did you get Webster to agree that?"

"I threatened him with sexual harassment."

"Sexual harassment, what's that?"

"That's funny, that's exactly what Webster said."

From the jukebox someone selected a record. The song, *The Most Beautiful Girl in the World* by Prince, filled the room.

Jill finished her beer. Still suffering from a hangover from the previous night, I drained my drink. My eyes glazed like melting ice as I bit my bottom lip. As Jill gave me a sympathetic smile, I had the curious feeling of being Mary Beth from the Cagney and Lacey TV detective programme.

★★★★

Five days later I got a telephone call.

"Is that Tony Bell?" It was a woman's voice, rasping like a heavy cigarette smoker.

"Who wants to know?"

"It's me, Tony, Irish Meg."

I exclaimed, "My God, it's been a few years!"

Meg rasped, "Over twenty, can you believe time can fly so fast?"

"How did you find my number?"

"A friend, I still have some, you know." She cleared her throat with a smoker's cough. "I read about your granddaughter. A sad affair, killing children is the biggest sin, Tony. I lost a girl, years ago, to some disease, so I know how painful it can be."

"Thanks for your sympathy, Meg. But I don't think you went to the trouble to find my number to pass on your condolences."

My caller made a sound in between a cough and a laugh. "You were always good, Tony. Too bloody good for the rozzers, you and me should have been business partners."

"I don't think so. Have you got something for me?"

There was a long pause before she declared, "Maybe."

"What do you mean, maybe?"

"I might have some info about the girls' killer."

I demanded, "What information?"

"I'll tell you face to face. Meet me in an hour at the old fish quay, I'll be waiting."

Before I could say anything else, the line went dead.

Rather than go via the tunnel, I drove to the ferry landing and after parking up my car, was soon on board crossing the river. I stood on the top deck of the ferry, letting the wind to sweep through my hair; clearing my head. Irish Meg use to be a working girl, prostituting with the many sailors that frequented a location called the Jungle. The place and the clientele had long disappeared, but during its heyday Irish Meg had passed on bits of information to me, for a small fee of course, plus an amnesty from prosecution from the vice squad.

It was a short walk from the north ferry terminal to the fish quay. As I arrived at the deserted market I saw her standing there, cigarette in hand, smoking like a chimney, as always, living on her nerves.

"She nodded and tossed the cigarette to the floor. She greeted me, "Long time, Tony."

I nodded back.

She said faintly, "You haven't changed much over the years."

I was in no mood for compliments or lies, so replied, "Pity I can't say the same for you." She must have been in her late forties, but her skin was deeply lined and her hair dull.

She gave an ironic smile and shrugged. "I'm afraid too many fags and late nights."

"I always thought when you were younger you were too good looking for the trade."

"It's in the blood. Did you know my grandmother as a child, was sold by her starving parents to a gentleman? Three silver half crowns for her virginity. Runs in the family you see."

"Are you still with Andrew?"

"Nah, he left me years ago. He works on the rigs, as a chef, which is funny when you consider he never cooked whilst he lived with me."

"What about your husband?"

"After Andrew stabbed him in the taxi, he believed he had grounds for a divorce and the judge agreed. Haven't seen him for years either. I believe he may have remarried, some woman from Norway; lives over there with him. So I've lost both my husband and my boyfriend. Life's a bitch."

"You live an interesting life. I hope you're not still working."

The smile turned into a larger grin. "Look at me, Tony. Who wants to sleep with their shagged-out grandmother? Besides, since the yards closed down and the fishing trawlers no longer visit, trade has all but dried up. It was always foreign seamen who needed the service. The locals don't need working girls, because the stupid tarts around here give it away free."

"Market forces, eh?"

"Still, there's always a niche, even in the most difficult of markets."

"A niche which I guess you've tapped into."

She almost sounded apologetic. "I run a small house, no more than three girls. Clients are mostly business men travelling through, or a few locals with urges they can't share with their girlfriends or wives."

"You make it sound like you are running a much-needed social service."

Meg nodded lazily, "Perhaps I am." A long pause, then Meg muttered, "I'm truly sorry about your Ellie, Tony."

She opened a metaphorical door, so I entered and asked, "What have you got, Meg?"

She paused before searching her pockets for a packet of cigarettes. She put one in her mouth and I waited whilst she struck a match and held the flame in cupped hands. Satisfied the tobacco was lit and taking a deep breath of tobacco, she said through an exhaled cloud of smoke, "Two nights ago, one of my girls had a customer. He asked for the youngest looking one. I actually have one girl, who is legal, but looks a little under age. You'd be surprised how many blokes go for that sort of thing."

I looked impatient.

She continued, "Well the John was a bit rough with her and afterwards, when he was having a shower, she decided a bit more money would be fair, so she went through his pockets." She paused, taking the opportunity to clear her chest with more coughing, "Actually I don't approve girls going through customers' pockets, gets me a bad reputation, but this particular girl has an expensive habit, if you get my drift." Another pause, whilst she dragged on the ciggy. Throwing it to the ground she declared, "She found a gold-coloured medallion in his pocket. It had a blue ribbon and the medal had on it an award for some skating competition. The girl's not too bright, Tony, and didn't realise the significance. Only when she told me the story, did we put two and two together."

I snapped, "Is he a regular John?"

"No, never seen him before."

I demanded, "Are you sure, Meg?"

She raised her right hand. "I promise on my mother's grave, it's the truth, Tony."

"So what do you know?"

"He drove a white van, I know that because he parked around the corner, but one of the other girls coming to work saw him."

I demanded, "Anything else?"

"He has a tattoo, on his arm."

"A tattoo?"

"Yes, some sort of knife, a dagger with some numbers, could be a birthday or the year he was born. The girl, as I said isn't too bright." Irish Meg swallowed, "Sorry that's all I have. I know the police are no longer looking for anyone, but I know for a fact most of them couldn't get laid in a brothel so what do they know? Perhaps this is important."

I said vigorously, "It is Meg. Thanks so much." I put my hand into my pocket and produced my wallet.

She immediately put her hand on my chest. "Tony, no, I'm not doing this for the victims, not money. Just make sure you get him, if he is the bastard that killed those two girls. Do that for ol' Irish Meg."

Chapter Twenty-Two

*W*hen I was young I accidently broke my brother's train set. I must have been four years of age. I rushed into the living room and the floor space was taken up with rail track and engines pulling coaches and goods trains. They were all moving in various directions, miraculously missing each other, colourful Hornby toys tooting away. Jack was lying on his stomach eagerly holding the controls in his hands. When I saw the whole system I just knew I wanted to travel on a train, they were, after all, passenger trains!

Before Jack could stop me I sat on one of the locomotives, breaking both the engine and the track. Like a modern-day Gulliver running amok, I rolled off and crashed into his main Lilliput station, breaking that too. Jack jumped up sobbing and ran to Mother whilst I scarpered up stairs, seeking sanctuary beneath my bed.

Mum made me apologise and Granddad did his best to repair the damage, but I sometimes think I broke more than a train set that day.

****

I've found a remote farm house in rural Northumberland. Not far from Morpeth, it's easy driving to the A1. It's more than a house it's a lair, a hide out where one can live without fear of nosy neighbours poking around. A person could feel safe here and live off the land, satisfying any primeval need for seclusion. It's where hate can fester free of distraction. Malevolent thoughts mature into malicious plans. Dreams turn into evil action, impulses into reality. Granddad told me evil exists when good men do nothing, but you can't do anything when evil is hidden.

This is where my monster lives. I watch him, as he goes about his business. Most hours he works out doing weight training, followed by a five-mile run. The half-starved dog survives in a kennel in the yard and chickens live in fear in the coop. The farm has rats and the monster uses a twelve-bore shotgun and shoots them. He's a good shot and the dog retrieves the dead animals and dumps them at her owner's feet. The shot vermin are then disposed of in a furnace.

The monster also shoots with his camera and takes countless pictures. He develops them in a dark room in the house. He has many photos of me, but now I'm dead, he takes pictures of other people. These are people I know and love. I bite my tongue and watch with horror as he develops long-range photos of Jack and Granddad and pins them to a corkboard. Some of the photos of Granddad show him talking to a lady at the old fishing quay. I recognise the location because he used to take me there when I was small.

When the rats are not available, the monster uses the photos as targets. I watch him in the yard, blasting pictures of my family to bits. I fear the monster is planning something bad and it involves them.

Days later I sit in the rear seat of his van, although he doesn't know I'm there as he drives out of the yard. I can see the reflection of his eyes in the rear mirror; they are dark, deep pools of madness. He heads for Hexham and I inhale deeply when he parks by another car near the river. Terrified, I recognise the car; its Granddad's. The monster opens his glove apartment and puts on a pair of gloves. He then takes out a long, pointed knife and handles the weapon with relaxed familiarity. It looks the deadly sort that's designed purely to kill people quickly and efficiently. Unable to breathe, I fear again for my family and feel there is nothing I can do.

I follow him down a path to the river where I see Granddad fishing on the riverbank. There is nobody else around. I sense Jack is further down the river and I turn and run towards him. I look over my shoulder; the monster is stealthily creeping up on Granddad, like a lion stalking prey, knife in hand.

Chapter Twenty-Three

I'm pleased I've told Jack about my suspicions that his sister's killer is still on the loose. Jack has focused his energy on hating this person. Whilst I don't condone hate, it does help to keep the pain at bay. Perhaps after the killer is captured, there will be time for pain; meanwhile, we focus on the task in hand.

Another week passed and Jack was searching the interior of the fridge, while his mother ate her breakfast, when I walked in. I wasn't alone.

Jack closed the fridge door and laughed, perhaps for the first time since the funeral as Judy exclaimed, "What have you got there, Dad?"

The answer was obvious as it was running around the kitchen wagging its tail. Nevertheless, I still answered, "It's a dog."

"I can see it's a dog." Judy scowled. "What's it doing here?"

Jack was on his knees and enthusiastically rubbing the dog's ears. He said to the dog, "Who's a bonny dog, then?"

I answered Judy wryly, "He's a retired copper, just like me. I picked him up last night from the police dog compound. He's looking for a retirement home."

"How will you look after him? He looks like a timber wolf, needing loads of upkeep." Judy sounded flabbergasted.

I replied, "It's a German Shepherd–Husky cross and it's not for me, it's for you."

Jack shouted, "Great."

Judy stood up from her chair. She said sharply, "He's not stopping here." She pointed at the dog with a finger. "Why do I need a dog?"

"His name is Sacha, he's very brave and is extremely well behaved."

"Have you gone mad, Dad? How will I look after a dog? Don't you think I've got enough on my plate at the moment?"

Jack pleaded, "I can take it for walks, Mum. It'll be great."

Judy wrapped her arms around her waist, exasperated. "Yes Jack, you'll take it for walks for the first few weeks and then," she snorted, "it'll be up to me to do it."

"No you won't," claimed Jack, "I promise I'll do it."

Judy replied, "Even when you're away at college?" She turned to me. "Why on earth do I need a pet?"

"It's not a pet. I got it for protection."

Judy sounded surprised, "Why do I need a dog for protection?"

Frustrated, I kept my voice level, "Because I had difficulty getting a hand gun."

She indicated towards me with an open hand. "What, you think I'm in danger, we, Jack and I are in danger?"

"Look, there's a mad man out there. Nobody is looking for him because he's a smart bastard and has hoodwinked the police. But face the facts, Judy, Ellie wasn't a random abduction, she was targeted. We still don't know the full motivation for the crime, so until we do, we have to assume we might all be in danger."

There was a pause before Judy sighed. "Please don't swear Dad." She inquired, "You're not just paranoid?"

"No, love, I'm not. Besides," I pointed to Sacha, "he's an old boy, but highly trained. He'll put his life on the line for you."

Judy shook her head vigorously, "I can't Dad. It's too early after Ellie. I don't think I can cope."

"You have to, love. You need it for protection. Besides, if we don't take it in, he may be put down."

Judy asked, "Put down where, the pit?"

Jack responded, "No Mam, he means the dog will be put to sleep." He sounded anxious.

"Your granddad is joking, Jack. Isn't that right, Dad?"

My bluff blown, I nodded. "Yup, but if you don't take the dog, someone else will."

Judy asked, "You really think we need protection?"
I nodded.

Judy shrugged and bent her head to the floor as she considered the situation. The dog sat and watched her with bright eyes, his tongue hanging from the corner of his mouth. Eventually she looked up and gave me her unconditional surrender. "So tell me, Dad. What have I got to do?"

I smiled, "You have to bond with him. You have to be top dog in this new pack; Jack has to be second top dog."

Judy sounded tired, "How do I go about that?"

"You, Judy, have to feed him. Provide the food, show who is boss."

"I have no dog food."

I put my hands in my pockets and produced two tins. "I have. In the car I've got his old bowls and blankets. He hasn't eaten since yesterday morning, so he's going to be really appreciative when you serve him breakfast."

They said at the police compound he was a very intelligent animal and to prove the point, Sacha wandered over to Judy. I think he could sense her sadness and nudged her hand with a wet nose. The dog recognised its new pack leader and rubbed himself against Judy's leg.

The pack leader gave a sigh and looking down said softly, "Hello Sacha. My name is Judy, welcome to your new home."

Jack looked at me and grinned as he winked.

Next day I took Jack fishing.

I thought it would be a good idea to let Judy and the dog spend a day together, bonding, whilst Jack and I did our own team building.

Jack sat in the front of the car with me as we drove along the country roads. "Do you think there'll still be fish, Granddad?"

I answered, "A few stragglers, perhaps. If there's no salmon, we might get brown trout."

"Talking about catching things, do you think we'll ever catch Ellie's killer?"

"Absolutely, Jack. We know he's smart and he'll think he's smarter than any of us, but he'll make mistakes. They all do, did I ever tell you about my first case as lead detective?"

"Don't think so."

"Two guys broke into a furniture shop on Ocean Road and tried to open the safe. They failed, so they carried the safe out with them; stole the safe. Can you imagine how heavy and how difficult that was?"

"So how did you catch them?"

I chuckled, "Next day I followed their footsteps in the snow to their flat in Vespasian Avenue. So occupied were they with the stolen safe, they forgot they were walking in crisp virgin snow."

Grinning, Jack turned to me and asked, "What did they get?"

I replied, "Six months plus a bad back and a hernia."

His face lit up.

Despite this not being the first time I had told the story, I laughed out loud as if I'd just heard it for the first time.

This had the promise of being a really good day.

Jack and I fished side by side from the bank for an hour, but nothing was biting apart from a few flies on our skin.

Jack turned, "Would you mind, Granddad, if I try further downstream?"

"Of course not son, just be careful."

I watched him wander down the side of the river. I loved the boy and he was starting to show signs of the adult he would become. I had many reasons to feel proud of my grandson. It was a pleasant day and it felt safe. I allowed my mind to go over the facts of Ellie's case as I cast my fly and spent the next half hour in deep contemplation. My mind was somewhere else, my internal radar wasn't working; my alert button was switched off.

I never heard him.

The first blow was to the back of the knee on my right leg. As I staggered forward the second blow came instantaneously to my kidneys. It was like being hit by a sledgehammer. I fell on all fours as the third blow, a well-aimed kick, struck me below the solar plexus knocking the wind out of me. I cried out with a sharp cry of pain as bile splashed at the back of my throat.

This was not a good fight. I'd been in scraps before, but each time I had been facing the aggressor when the punches started. Also, it's my experience few people really know how to fight properly. I've seen supposedly hard men, who when it came to the punch boxed like girls. This was different. First of all I'd been attacked from behind and therefore had no defence. Second, this guy knew what he was doing.

Another kick to my ribs, but this one was softer, not executed to hurt, but performed to spin me over onto my back.

I grunted as he pounced onto my chest, pinning me to the ground, his eyes filled with hate. Sitting on my chest, I struggled to breathe. I could smell his insanity, a rancid odour. He produced a long dagger and lifted it above his head.

His voice was calm but he couldn't disguise the sneer. "We're going to have some fun, Tony." He leaned forward and whispered, "I'm going to kill you, because I can and because I want to, also because it'll give me great pleasure. Then I'm going to kill Jack and finally your daughter. Neither of them will die quickly; each will be a painful death. I'm going to abuse them in ways that are beyond even your imagination. But first, I have to get rid of you, because you're just a pain in the arse."

My eyes bulging, I screamed as the knife went even higher before flashing down, towards my jugular.

Chapter Twenty-Four

I ran like I'd never run before, like the wind, speeding towards Jack. I saw him in the distance; fishing from the bank, oblivious of the danger Granddad was in. He looked in a good mood. The grief of my death was at that moment put to one side and I could hear him whistling. Granddad's idea of bringing in a dog to the family was helping. Jack was reeling in his line. Nobody else was around, even the birds seemed to have flown, no doubt frightened by the monster now on their territory.

I yelled, "JACK!"

My voice faded away on the breeze. Jack couldn't hear me. His line was now fully wound on his reel and he lifted his rod vertical to cast when I screamed again, "JACK!"

This time he stopped and turned, a startled look on his face. I ran forward a few yards and screamed again, "Granddad is in danger!"

He couldn't hear me, not in the conventional sense, but something triggered in his mind. He hesitated a few seconds *before starting to run back along the riverbank. We must have been about three hundred yards from Granddad, but Jack was fit. I ran alongside him, urging him on. Still carrying his rod, Jack seemed to respond because he soon turned a corner and saw the attacker fifty yards away, sitting on Granddad's chest. The monster was shouting at Granddad and then started to raise his knife.*

It was too far to run, we were too late. My hands came to my face; I was about to watch Granddad being stabbed to death.

I screamed again in despair as Jack, quick as lightning, started casting his fly. Swoosh, swoosh, swoosh and in an instant he had control of the fifty yards of line that were dancing out through the air towards the target. Jack had a large fly on with an oversized hook and the tackle flew through the air striking the monster in the left eye just as the knife started its descent. Jack expertly pulled on his rod as the lure moved over the monster's eye. The point and barb sunk deeply into the soft tissue, catching hold and when Jack gave one final jerk, the snagged eye was removed like a cork from a bottle. The eye and hook flew through the air.

I screamed again and then again, but the second cry was a scream of relief.

The stunned monster also let out a terrible yell before rolling after his eye and falling off Granddad. Granddad turned the opposite way and staggered up. Jack ran towards him as the traumatised monster, holding his bloody face with one hand, his knife in the other, turned and staggered back towards his car. Granddad was too injured to give chase and Jack's concern was for him. The troll escaped, leaving blood stains and his eye behind.

Later Jack would tell our mother this was the best catch he'd EVER made.

I watched as the one-eyed monster drove erratically down minor roads, avoiding the traffic. Holding a handkerchief to his injury, he squinted through the tears in his good eye, trying to hold the road, forcing one cyclist off the road and into the ditch.

Gasping and swearing, the dazed predator eventually arrived at the isolated farmhouse and his dog ran up to him. The monster stumbled from the van, leaving the door ajar and the poor dog got a severe kicking for its troubles. Inside, the injured troll pulled out kitchen drawer after kitchen drawer, and scattered the contents over the floor, until he found a first aid kit boxed in camouflage with a large red cross on it. Taking a syringe, he pulled on a bottle of morphine and injected himself in the neck to deaden the pain, before washing the gash with iodine and dressing it expertly with clean bandages. He spat onto the floor and being satisfied he'd done everything he could; he took another shot of morphine and staggered to bed with a bottle of whisky. Lying on top of the unmade bed he took three large slugs of the whisky before he fell into a stupor.

I pointed with my hand and shouted at him, "I told you not to mess with my family." He couldn't hear, of course, but it did feel good that the nasty monster was in some pain.

I whispered to myself, "Thanks Jack. Thank you for saving Granddad's life."

Chapter Twenty-Five

I screamed as I've never screamed before. From the depth of my lungs the sound rose up, strong enough to start an avalanche. I thought no one could scream louder, but I was wrong. I was facing certain death when Jack's lure suddenly flashed across my attacker's face, surprising both of us. The hook sank into his eye like the fangs of a Hammer film Dracula biting into a maiden's neck.

I watched as his features twisted in a horrified contortion, and as the popped eye was dragged away blood splattered on my face. An ear-splitting and sickening scream tore past his lips and the knife, half way on its journey to obliterate me, never reached its destination. Both of his hands went to his injury as he spun off me. Still screaming like a wounded animal, he disappeared, possibly for all I know, back to hell, from where he had escaped.

"Are you all right, Granddad?" Panting, Jack ran up to me, his chest heaving like a piston engine. "Are you okay?"

I was bent over and unsure which part of my body hurt the most. I felt as if I had just walked away from a head-on collision. I twisted my head up and looked at Jack. "Did you just do what I think you did?"

He sounded apologetic. "I couldn't get back in time; I didn't know what to do."

I would have laughed if it didn't hurt so much. "Jack, lad, you did well. You've just saved your gramp's life; I don't think I've ever been so close to death before." I managed to straighten my back and ignoring the pain said, "Bloody hell, son, you're a hero, a bloody hero."

Jack looked a little embarrassed. "I'm not in any trouble am I?"

I laughed through the pain this time. "I've told you Jack, you're a hero. Is it still on your line?"

He asked stiffly, "The eye?"

Humour flickered briefly as I replied, "Aye, the eye."

Jack gave a little shiver. "Yes, it's a little gruesome, but it's still there."

"Just as well you came back when you did, otherwise I'd be dead."

Jack looked uncertain. "Granddad, I just knew you were in trouble, that's why I ran back."

"Did you hear something?"

Jack sniffed, "No, I just knew you were in trouble."

I smiled. "It's called intuition, Jack." I put my hand on his shoulder. "All good coppers have it. I must have handed some down to you."

Jack continued his uncertain look. "It's just that… Oh, it's nothing. You're right, it was intuition."

Jack helped me hobble back to the car, and at the first phone box I called Jill Adams and told her what happened. She put out an APB to all hospitals in a wide area asking them to report any emergencies involving a lost eye. I finished by saying I was coming in with some evidence.

Just over an hour later, Jack and I sat opposite Jill in her office. She grimaced and dropping her voice, asked, "Is that it?" She indicated to the object on her desk.

Jack replied, "Yes, that's the eye."

I added dryly, "Aye the eye was removed by my new partner, Jack Peach, fisherman extraordinary." I could smell her perfume, subtle and expensive.

Jill retained her frown. "And just what exactly do you want me to do with it?"

I responded, "I take it there's been no reports from any A&E about the injured party."

"No and I doubt if there will be. This guy's too clever to walk into a hospital, eye missing or not."

I concurred. "You're right, Jill, but can't we use this eye for DNA sampling?"

Jill leaned forward, "Tony, we don't yet have a national database, we've only just started to collect the information. The samples we have only run into hundreds. I would be very surprised if our man is in the files."

"This guy will HAVE a record. You don't go from nothing to a multi-murderer in one step. I also guess the authorities will have been taking unofficial DNA samples for some time. Try a comparison on that database."

Jill let out a long, quiet breathe. "I'll see what I can do, Tony. Just don't get excited and have high expectations." She collected her thoughts then asked, "How do we know this is our man and not some random attack by some mad local?"

I sat back in my chair. "He knew my name and Jack's. No doubt this is our man. Now he's injured he'll be even more dangerous, but more liable to make mistakes. If you provide me some mugshots I'll see if I can ID him. We might just get lucky."

An hour passed during which Jack and I viewed various faces of known criminals, but we came up blank. I hadn't really expected to find anything; it was just another box that required ticking. I smiled sadly at Jack. "Sorry to put you through this, son."

"It's all right. I'm happy to help with anything really to catch this guy.

Jill had left us alone to look through the photo files and she now returned, inquiring, "Anything?"

I replied, "I'm afraid not."

Jill's eyes narrowed. "It was worth a shot." She looked again at the eye on her desk and turned to Jack, "And well done you, young man."

Jack replied sincerely, "Thank you, Jill." He sounded quite adult.

I said, "I'm taking Jack to the canteen for coffee. Why don't you get Sweetman to take the evidence to the lab boys and join us for a cuppa?"

Jill smiled, "You're insufferable, Tony. If you're trying to wind up Webster by using the canteen I have to tell you, it's his day off." She laughed out loud. "Make mine milk and no sugar, I'll be along in a few minutes."

Chapter Twenty-Six

*T*he hairs on the back of my neck lifted. I realised I had communicated in some way with Jack. The knowledge made me excited. Normally people communicate using the conscious part of the brain, so if I say, "Hi", another person hears via their ears and their alert mind processes the information and responds. Jack hadn't heard me through his ears, he'd heard me much deeper in his mind, perhaps even in his subconscious. It really didn't matter, the fact was little me, little DEAD me had communicated with my brother.

How awesome is that? Who else could I speak to? The question made me excited. I had the sensation my heart was fluttering like the wings of a humming bird, which is strange if you think about it. Can dead people feel their hearts? I giggled at the notion.

I decided I'd been alone for too long. Ignoring the feeling I was being naughty, my legs trembled as I closed my eyes. I whispered his name to the wind and then, like a mantra, kept repeating it.

I felt the wind, moving my hair ever so gently. Was I flying or just floating?

I waited until I could no longer feel the gentle breeze before opening my eyes. It was dark and as my eyes grew accustomed to the light, I saw I was in a bedroom. Awestruck, I walked to the side of the bed and looked down. He had his pyjama bottoms on but his top was bare. I could see his chest. Already the muscle was forming, changing him from adolescent to adult. Adam was two years older than me. He was a fourteen year-old boy asleep in his bedroom with the perfectly-shaped lips I'd never kissed. I crawled onto the bed and lay beside him, cuddling up to his back.

I whispered, "Hello, Adam." He couldn't hear me, of course, but perhaps his mind could in its deep sleep. I closed my eyes and cried out, "Adam I love you. Please dream about me!"

A sweet dream on the beach; are dreams real? I don't know, but this one did feel real. Whose dream was it? It doesn't matter. All that matters is what happened. We were the only people on the sands as we strolled along hand in hand, Adam's chest turning brown under the sun. We came to an outcrop of rocks on the beach and sat by the water's edge creating our own little space, our own world.

Adam said, "When I was a little boy, I played right here. I pretended this was a fort and I had to shoot at imaginary bad people who were attacking it."

"I use to play around here, too. Pity we didn't meet up then."

Adam turned his face to me. "Ellie, I'm so sorry what happened to you. Did you know I cried when I heard the news?"

I stuttered, "No, I had no idea. Why did you cry?"

"Because I was so sad, I liked you a lot and hoped one day, when we were older perhaps you would be my girlfriend."

I cried out with happiness, "Adam, of course I would have been your girl!"

"I asked your mum if I could help carry the coffin at the funeral. I thought she would say no, but she just smiled and nodded. I cried a little at the funeral. Couldn't help myself, I'd never lost a friend or anybody I knew before. It was very hard. Did you know lots of the other pupils at school cried too?"

I could see Adam was getting sad at the memory, so I got on my knees and touched his leg, saying, "Adam, we're in a dream, let's not waste it being unhappy."

"Will I remember the dream? Will I remember?"

I felt a blush creep up my face and whispered. "I hope so, I truly hope so."

"Lots of people are saying Jimmy your coach didn't kill you, is that right?"

"No, Jimmy was not my killer. The man who wanted to kill me is still at large and my granddad is going to catch him."

"I hope he does."

"When I played here as a girl, this was a fairy castle not a fort. I kept imaginary horses here and I was the beautiful princess. My brother would always spend his time catching crabs, but I invented a whole new world, where anything was possible."

He gave me a mischievous smile. "You know if this is a dream, anything is possible, we can do anything we want."

I nodded my head wildly; I felt my heart would burst.

His throat sounded dry as he asked, "Should we?"

"Do IT, you mean?" I felt incredibly naughty, yet something inside reminded me that had I lived I would have grown into an adult. Perhaps this was my one opportunity to be that person I could never be, the grown-up Ellie. I wanted to taste and encounter some of the future that had been so cruelly stolen from me. I wanted so much to experience the thrill of being a grown woman. Also, nobody can be judgemental of a dream. Nobody.

His answer hardly passed his lips. "Yes."

My eyes could not have been wider. "Why not, it's a dream. Nothing more, no reality or consequence for our actions, we can do what we want."

"It'll be my first time."

I looked deeply into his eyes. "It'll be my first and only time."

I let Adam take my clothes off and watched him as he removed his pants. I went moist with anticipation, like the morning dew, and I thought no need for condoms in dreams. I suppressed another giggle as Adam's penis looked bigger than any banana Miss Hawley ever showed in the class.

I lay back on the sand and Adam lay beside me, his fingers caressing the inside of my leg, his feather-light touch sending me into joy as my body jolted.

He muttered, "I can't wait, Ellie," his voice dazed with desire. He climbed on top of me, pinning me to the sand, his face flushed and I gave a wide smile to let him know it was okay. Our lips came together and we kissed. With the heavenly touch of his lips I opened up like a flower. I gasped as he entered me and we were joined as one.

I cried out, "Adam I love you." A tear trickled out from my eye.

Adam grunted and breathed in short gasps, unable to control his passion.

I felt my lips on his neck; primeval urges had me sucking at his salty, masculine skin. I closed my eyes, tight shut. Happiness flowed through me as goose bumps rose all over my skin and a surge of pleasure rushed through me.

I cried out again, "Adam, I love you," as I rode the crest of a wave.

Slowly the world came back and when I opened my eyes I was back in Adam's room, standing by his bed. Adam was still asleep but now on his back. He looked serene lying on top of his duvet and I noticed two things. Adam had a damp patch on his pyjamas around his groin. I could heart Miss Hawley's voice in my head, "It's very common for young boys to have wet dreams, nothing unusual about it."

However the other thing WAS unusual. On the left side of Adam's neck he had a love bite. It would still be there in the morning and he would be terribly confused as he hid it from his parents. Years in the future, when Adam is an old man he will finally tell his grandchildren about the night he dreamed about a dead girl and how he awoke up with a hickey on his neck. He won't mention the fact the dream was a wet one, but the incident will mean I will live forever in his mind. I wish I could tell someone, especially my best friend, Talia. Yeah, I know it's spooky, but I'm only twelve years old so I'm allowed to be naughty sometimes and it was only a dream. I'm not sure *when my smile will eventually leave my face; perhaps it'll last longer than Adam's hickey.*

Two nights later, I found myself in another bedroom. It was my brother Jack's. He was wrapped in his duvet, warm and snug. I crept up to the bed and, getting on all fours, kneeled down beside his sleeping form. I paused and looked at his face. My brother Jack won't dance at my wedding but in ten years' time, I'll be looking down at his.

I decided to surprise him.

Putting my hands under the bed I swept and searched by touch. I soon found what I was looking for, a shoebox. The box was filled with Daddy's souvenirs. Most of it was military cap badges, medals and some photos. I tipped out the contents in the middle of the room. Before my death, had I done such a thing, Jack would have got really angry and gone ballistic, as Granddad would say. Tomorrow morning he's just going to be confused, then conclude he'd been sleep walking. The moment he puts the stuff back in the box he will crack open the case. Jack will start to discover who my monster really is.

Before I left I touched my brother's forehead. I whispered, "I love you Jack. You have nothing to be sorry for. Thank you, Jack, thank you so much. Take care of Mummy, tell her I love her so much and I'll be watching all of you. Also tell Granddad I'm happy."

Jack grunted in his sleep.

He is going to grow up into a nice person and he's going to happily marry my best friend, Talia. Their first child will be a girl and they'll call her Ellie, after me.

How do I know such things? I do, I just do. It's really wicked.

Chapter Twenty-Seven

I had slept the last few nights at Judy's. The dog seemed to resent my presence, but hell, I was more family than him. The trouble was he didn't seem to know that fact. We lived side by side like two cellmates, reluctant captives thrown together by events rather than friendship. Judy was right; he was more wolf than dog.

It was early morning and I was putting the kettle on when Jack walked into the kitchen. He looked as white as a ghost.

I asked anxiously, "What's wrong, Jack?"

He looked like he was ready to faint. "The tattoo, the one the murderer has."

"Yes?"

"You said it was a dagger with some numbers."

"Yes."

Jack put a silver cigarette lighter on the kitchen table. "This is my Dad's. Look at the insignia on the side."

I picked up the lighter and saw the dagger and the number 45.

Jack's said, "It's my Dad's regiment. The Royal Marines, four-five Commando, I think that's what the tattoo is. It's their insignia."

I flicked the lighter; it sparked but of course the wick was dry. I noticed my hand was shaking. "Bloody hell, Jack, this is incredible. This might be the key to the whole investigation." I looked at the lighter, feeling a grin cover my lips. I continued, "I think you're bloody right. Good grief, it's possible our man might be an ex-commando. I think you've just brought us a lot closer to Ellie's killer."

Judy walked in with an empty cup in her hand. "What's going on?" Beside her stood the dog, its tail wagging.

I said, "Our Jack's just brought this down." I showed her the lighter.

A shadow of a smile crossed Judy's lips as she recognised her late husband's property. "That's Jack's, he liked using a lighter when he smoked." She looked at the two of us. "Gave it up when young Jack was born."

I asked, "Did you know it has his regiment insignia on it?"

"Wouldn't surprise me, he was mad about the regiment, especially in the early days. Band of brothers and all that. I used to joke, my husband has a mistress and she's called the Royal Marines."

Jack interrupted, "Mum, look at the insignia."

"What's special about it?"

"Remember what Granddad said, Ellie's killer has a tattoo…"

"Of course," Judy gasped, bringing a fist to her mouth. "You don't think it's someone Jack knew, do you?"

Catching a whiff of the dog as I stepped over him, I said, "Not sure what we know. But it's a lead, and I wouldn't be surprised if the guy who hit me had some sort of military training. He was good, too good, to have learned fighting from the streets. I'm going to see Jill, bring her up to date."

Judy turned to Jack. "What made you think of it?"

Jack shrugged. "When I awoke this morning, a load of Dad's things was all over the floor. I must have done it in my sleep or something. I was putting them back in the box when the lighter seemed to stick to my hand like a leech. It was then I saw the insignia."

Judy smiled. "Did you say you were tidying your room, Jack?" She looked at me, forcing a thin smile onto her sad lips. "It seems my son is growing up at last."

Jack asked enthusiastically, "Should I go with you, Granddad?"

"No, Jack, best if you stay with your mum. Better take the dog for a walk first. My copper's nose detects the animal is very close to doing his business."

The sky was doughy grey, the air chilly and granular. It was a Tuesday morning as I drove down town, or as the locals would say, "down street". Autumn seemed extended, winter yet to arrive. I was excited; young Jack had certainly found gold. My intuition screamed out that he was right. There was a connection, although tenuous at that moment and I thought the investigation was back on track. We would find our man, the rabid animal that had ripped our family apart.

Jill hadn't yet reported for duty, so DC Sweetman got me a coffee whilst I waited in her office. The coffee smell drifting up my nose was good. My senses, which had dulled since Jimmy's murder, seemed to have sharpened with the discovery of the lighter. I was buoyant. The terrible feeling of impotency had reached its high-tide mark and was now ebbing away. I felt years younger. I stared through the plume of steam rising from the coffee at the far wall. I could hear the bustle of things going on behind me, the familiar sound of a busy police station. My brain was sharp and occasionally I missed the action, but life is what you make it and this is what I had made of my life.

As I finished my cup of coffee, the door opened and Jill walked in.

She gave a genuine smile. "You're early, Tony. What have you got?"

I waited until she took her coat off and was sitting down at her desk before I replied, "I think our suspect is ex-commando."

Her eyebrows shot up, "Wow, that's a big leap, how so?"

"The tattoo, I think it's the insignia of four-five Commando; the regiment Ellie's dad was in."

Jill frowned, "You think there's a connection?" She put her head to one side.

"I'd bet my pension on there being some sort of connection." I leaned forward, "I take it you haven't found anything via the DNA?"

Jill shook her head with a disappointed look on her face.

"Do the army have a DNA database?"

"I think the Commandos are part of the Navy, Tony. But I doubt if any of the forces have a DNA database. We do think we know the suspect's blood group, but as it's the most common blood type, it isn't going to help."

"So what do we do?"

"I'll get Sweetman onto it. Make some inquiries, come back after lunch, I might have something for you."

I gave a slight nod. "It was young Jack, who cracked it. Found a cigarette lighter belonging to his Dad. It had the regimental insignia on it and he put two and two together, smart kid."

Jill gave the warmest smile as she reached for the phone. "Just like his granddad."

I spent the next few hours walking along the shore heading for a landmark called Trow Rocks. I fantasised Ellie was walking alongside me and I was answering her many questions. How do bees fly? How does television work? Is there a God? Hopefully, she has the answer to the last question by now, or does the mystery continue to the other side, if there is another side?

Jack said the lighter had stuck to his hand like a leech. I fantasised Ellie had been there to help her brother solve the case in some sort of spiritual way. It was a nice thought, but the old cynic in me knew it was all rubbish. Dead is dead, 'life is not a dress rehearsal' etcetera...

Leaving the beach, I saw a butterfly in the long grass. I smiled; it was very late in the season to see such a sight, was it a sign or even a miracle? Was Ellie or heaven trying to tell me something?

I wished I could believe, but the butterfly was just an aged lone survivor in a hostile environment, the exception proving the rule. A bit like me really.

Two o'clock and I sat down in Jill's office again. DC Sweetman was there with her, his note pad open.

He had a weary look on his face that was not a good sign.

Jill turned towards him. "Give us your report, Peter."

"Yes, mam." He began, "The Army wasn't as helpful as I'd expected."

Jill corrected him. "Navy, Peter, not the Army."

He shrugged. "Anyway, the tattoo could well be on the arm of any ex-commando, not necessarily from the four-five. It's not actually a uniform badge, but what they call a formation flash. Anybody who completes the commando course is allowed to wear the insignia, without needing to be in the Royal Marines. Others, from other parts of the armed forces, sometimes do the course to sharpen their soldiering skills, I suppose."

I scratched the back of my neck, ignoring my sinking feeling. I asked, "Anything else?"

"Well if it is the four-five, their headquarters are in Arbroath, Scotland. They specialise in arctic warfare and living off the land, eating grass and squirrels. Hard bastards, I bet."

"Thank you, Peter." Jill turned to me. "There may be hundreds of people with this tattoo. We don't even know if it's genuine or something picked up by a wannabe in a tattoo parlour."

I retorted, "This guy's the real thing. I can tell by the way he handled himself. It has to be the four-five, it's the only connection we have between the family and him." I turned to Sweetman. "Is there anything else?"

"I got the name and address of a retired NCO from the four-five. A bit of an expert on the history of the corps." He wagged a finger from side to side. "Mustn't call it a regiment, bloke on telephone nearly bit my ear off over that gaff."

I said incredulously, "You have a name?"

"Yes, McDonald, retired eight years ago after nearly twenty- seven years in the Marines. Lives in Leeds."

I caught the three-thirty from Newcastle mainline station. It was the King's Cross special and if I changed at York, it would get me to Leeds in just over two hours. I realised I hadn't eaten all day, so stood at the buffet car eating a sandwich and drinking another coffee. Jill called ahead to McDonald so he would be expecting me.

At twenty minutes past six I knocked on his door.

The address was a rather modest three-bedroom terraced house. McDonald looked in his late forties and still had a slight Scottish burr to his voice. The house smelled faintly of mothballs and dust. He turned off the BBC news and asked me to sit on his sofa.

He asked, "Would you like a drink, whisky maybe?"

"It's a bit early," I replied without offending.

"It's never too early for a wee one, Mr Bell." I watch him pour himself a single malt. He was a big man who still looked fit and had the stance of a retired soldier. As he sat down his face was a blank expression, and I wondered when the pullover he was wearing had last been cleaned. He eventually said, "I guess you're wondering what a highlander is doing living in Leeds."

I shrugged.

"My wife was a local lass; loved her to bits. When I retired, we moved back here. Unfortunately 'the best laid plans of mice and men' go belly up; she died three years ago. Like that wee doggie at Greyfriars, I feel reluctant to leave her grave, so I stay."

There was a pause, so I said, "His name was Bobby." I hesitated again, "The wee dog, his name was Bobby."

He allowed a dry smile to cross his lips. "I knew that, Mr Bell, Greyfriars Bobby. Is it not an ironic thing that ma name's Bobby, too?"

He looked at me with intense eyes, wondering heaven knows what. I said eventually, "My name is Tony."

He took a swig of his whisky. "Well, what can I do for you, Tony?"

"Did you read about the murder of two girls up north?"

He raised his eyebrows. "Aye, I did. Sad affair. Such young lasses. The fella responsible took his own life, is that not so?"

I shook my head. "I don't think so; the guy who killed himself was, in my opinion, murdered also. Set up as a patsy by the killer."

"Was he now?"

"Yes, to throw the police off the scent, so to speak."

"So how can I help?"

"I believe the man responsible is an ex-commando, possibly from the four-five."

He looked surprised. "My old corps. What makes you think the murderer is an ex member?"

"He has a tattoo of a dagger and some numbers; I think the numbers are four-five."

McDonald gave a wry smile and rolled up the sleeve on his left arm. "Like this one." He had a tattoo showing a six-inch dagger with the number '45' underneath.

I nodded.

"The majority of the Royal Marines in our corps has this tattoo, including those non-members who completed our course, not forgetting the 'wannabes'. It's a badge of honour. You're looking at hundreds of people, even thousands, people who fought in World War II onwards. It'll be like looking for a needle in a haystack."

I said bitterly, "A needle in a haystack is better odds than we had yesterday."

"What makes you so sure he was in the four-five?"

"The first girl killed – I'm her grandfather. Her late father was in the four-five and I think there is as connection. It was not a random attack."

"She was your granddaughter? I'm sad to learn that. What was her daddy's name?"

I replied solemnly, "His name was Jack Peach."

Bobby drained his glass and went for a refill. As he poured he said, "I know the name. He was one of those killed in the South Atlantic, is that right?"

"Yes, killed in action."

He sat down in front of me. "I had the reputation of being a bit of an anorak in the corps, being big on the history. The four-five has seen action from Aden to Zanzibar; good men, highly trained. But like any organisation you'll get the occasional bad egg. Not everyone who wears the green beret deserves to wear it." He dropped his head for a minute and as he raised it again asked, "What do you think the motivation was, then?"

"It's sexual or revenge or a toxic mix of the two. Something must have happened in the past, a trigger, to unleash this monster."

"Sometimes, Tony, we have to make monsters and turn men into animals, otherwise they couldn't do what is required of them."

I replied bitterly, "The Royal Marines doesn't train men to kill little girls, Bobby."

"Aye, you're right" He sat back in his chair, contemplating. Eventually he said, "Would you mind if I make a telephone call? Even amongst a group of monsters an ogre will stand out."

He left the room and was away for about ten minutes. When he entered the room again he looked triumphant. "I've just called an old friend in the military police; seems your son-in-law came up on their computer."

Incredulously I stuttered, "What? Jack was in trouble?"

"Not trouble, Tony, it seems your Jack was a chief prosecution witness in a court martial, a big military tribunal."

I gasped, "When?"

"1981."

"What happened?"

"The four-five had just got back to Scotland after some very intense training in arctic warfare in Norway. I was away on special duties, doing ma bit for Queen and country. As usual, the lads went to town and let their hair down. In other words, they got blind drunk."

"So what happened?"

"Your Jack beat up and I mean, really beat up, a sergeant. Gave him a really good hammering."

"I thought you said Jack was a chief prosecution witness?"

McDonald smiled, "Aye he was. I remember it now, a private beating up a sergeant and getting away with it. Jack became a bit of a legend in the corps."

"So how did he get away with it?"

"He stopped the sergeant in the middle of a rape. A local lass, not yet twelve, still at school; your Jack heard her scream and found the assault behind a stone wall. He leapt over and put the boot in, kicking the shit out of the son-of-a-bitch. I believe the girl's family was very grateful, although the girl was half dead and traumatised. She was infected with an STD and suffered two broken arms in the attack. I believe she couldn't speak for a year afterwards."

"What happened to the sergeant?"

"The Government kept the military trial out of the national news. Case was held in camera. But the sergeant got ten to fifteen years and was dishonourably discharged from the corps. The first few years were in a military prison. I bet his life was hell. Then he was transferred to a civilian prison, where he served the rest of his custodial sentence." Bobby McDonald smiled. "Do you want to hear the good news?" His eyes grew larger.

I nodded, although I guessed what was coming and it wasn't necessarily good news.

"The bastard was released twelve months ago, so there's a really good chance this is your man."

My mouth was dry, my hands shaking. "Does he have a name, this sergeant?" I sounded impatient.

"Aye, he does; his name's Robert Monk. I bet he goes by the name of Bobby, same as me, fucking pervert." He stopped. There was no more information to give. Smiling thinly he then said, "Now, Tony, will ya be having that wee whisky now?"

I nodded, "Not a wee one, Bobby. Make it a very large one."

Chapter Twenty-Eight

*W*hen Jack woke up and found the mess on the floor he looked befuddled. He no longer had a younger sister to shout at and blame. Couldn't be Mum or Granddad and as the door was still closed it was unlikely to be the new dog. He rubbed his head, like someone who just witnessed a great trick by a magician and had no idea how it was done. I beamed a smile as he scratched his bottom and sat on the floor before starting to replace the objects back in the box. When he picked up the lighter, Jack played with it, flicking it and causing it to spark. As he leaned towards the shoebox, I put my hand over his. He couldn't feel me, of course, but he did do an abrupt stop. He turned over his fist and opened his hand; the insignia was face up and as he recognised the significance the blood drained from his face.

Jack ran down stairs to see Granddad. I finished putting away the rest of the things and put the box back under the bed. Jack wouldn't even notice when he'd returned. Brothers can be really thick about this sort of things. If I had moved his *magazines that were also hidden under the bed, I bet he would have noticed!*

When Granddad walked along the shoreline, I walked beside him. I talked to him and I think his mind picked up the words, because he talked back, through his mind, although he thought he was only imagining the conversation. I love my Granddad, and I'm sorry he won't see me marry. It's every granddad's dream to see their grandchild marry. But I'll be in his dreams in other ways. Granddad doesn't know yet, but there will be a time when he'll know I'm at rest, happy in my heaven. I know my heaven seems to be a dowdy, dull building, but if there is a God, it must be some sort of paradise. I remain optimistic and that's a big word for a twelve year old, even one who's all grown-up and has kissed a boy.

Granddad missed his return train from Leeds. He telephoned his lady police friend with the monster's name and then had a large whisky with kind Mr McDonald. Then he had another one followed by another. Granddad hadn't eaten much that day, so by the time Crime Watch *was on TV, he was fast asleep on Mr McDonald's settee. Mr McDonald finished off the bottle before he too fell asleep. Next day, Granddad woke up with a bad head and to the smell of bacon being fried. After a hearty breakfast and lots of coffee, he had a spring in his step by the time he reached home a few hours later. He even asked Jack to make him another cup of coffee and another bacon sandwich.*

In my new world, I'm caught between heaven and earth. I sometimes feel like Alice in Wonderland as I'm full of awe at the things I see, and I tiptoe around so not to disturb people I love. Other times I think I'm like Little Red Riding Hood in a world full of unknown dangers, with a big, bad wolf ready to eat and devour me. In either world I know there is no Prince Charming to rescue me. I'm on my own, alone, full of wonder yet still afraid.

There's no fairy-tale ending for me and when I think about that it makes me sad.

I watch the monster become more of a recluse, never straying too far from his lair. He digs up worms and makes an omelette with them and eats greedily. Sometimes he kills a rabbit or a wood pigeon. He gathers berries from trees and his drinking water comes from a nearby stream. He shaves his head and keeps his hair cut short, more like stubble than a hairstyle.

The dog gets thinner and walks around with drooping ears and a low tail. It's becoming more difficult to distinguish between the two which is the animal and which the owner. The monster's injured eye slowly heals and he no longer wears a bandage. He has one mirror at the farm and one day after looking at his image he howled like a feral cat, took his shotgun and blasted the mirror. His pain runs deep and that's a good thing.

When a new Crime Watch was broadcast on TV, his name was mentioned and the presenter said the police were looking for him, but the public should not approach. The monster cackled an evil laugh that made his dog wail.

One morning he took from the fridge an old packet of Rollos. Taking two chocolates from the half eaten tube, he injected some fluid using a syringe into each of the caramel centres. Taking one doctored candy, he walked outside calling his dog. The collie's ears were down and the poor animal's eyes were wretched.

"Good girl." He playfully threw the chocolate sweet towards the hungry dog, which caught the treat in mid-air with a half-hearted leap. The ravenous canine chewed furiously. The monster folded his arms across his chest, feet apart, watching with a cold dull eye and a sour look on his face. Within a minute the dog was coughing, its chest heaving with a whooping sound as it tried to vomit. The distressed animal bent its forelegs and tried to reject the poison. Its last few moments were agony and it knew the person who should have looked after it had conspired to kill it. It took three to four minutes for the collie to die. The monster checked his wristwatch and seemed satisfied with his test, for that was what it was.

Back inside the house, the monster carefully wrapped up the other poisoned chocolate in a tissue and put it back in the fridge. I wasn't sure what his plan was, but as anxiety flowed through my body, I just knew it was evil and concerned my family.

So my monster now has a name. I can't speak it or write it, because that makes him seem almost human. He's not human; he's a MONSTER, a troll, fiend, brute, ogre, beast and a tyrant slime ball. Worse than the child catcher, worse than the worst thing that's ever lived. I hate him. He killed poor Mary, poor Jimmy and I'm going to kill him. If you don't believe it, you just watch me. Just as David, in the Bible, had his sling to kill his monster, I need a weapon to kill mine. The thought of what my weapon will be occupies my mind.

Chapter Twenty-Nine

It was early evening. Outside the sky was studded with rain-washed stars as the rain eased to a thin drizzle.

Jill had just come off duty and we sat opposite each other in a booth in a local coffee and ice cream parlour. She nodded to the Italian owner's son, who now ran the business and he brought over two cups of coffee. A family-run business for over a hundred years, the place was stuck in the décor of the Sixties but lots of people, including myself, liked it. Minchella's coffee house was a constant in a fast-changing world. In fact it was the place I'd met my wife when we were still teenagers.

Jill leaned over the table, keeping her voice low. "Webster's not too happy. This Robert Monk, if he is our man, makes Webster look like an idiot with his original statement to the top boss."

I replied, "Webster is an idiot. The killer designed an elephant trap, not too subtle, and Webster jumped in feet first." Jill's face was without expression. I waited for her response but when none was forthcoming I asked, "Have you anything more on Monk?"

"As you said, he was released twelve months ago, after doing a thirteen-year stretch. His probation officers tell me he's disappeared; they have no idea where he is. Do you know what they called him? 'Rasputin the mad monk.' Rather appropriate I think."

I rubbed my eye and asked, "What about the military?"

"They were at first reluctant to pass on any info'. But eventually I found a young Captain who came clean. He told me the records show Monk was a nasty piece of work. There had been another rape of a young girl in Cyprus in 1979, during some commando field training. Monk was charged, but there was no hard evidence to tie him to it. The Captain suggested he might have done some covert work with the SAS, special ops and all that. "She looked concerned. "Monk's very dangerous, Tony. He's highly trained and possibly insane. Anyway I've talked to the police liaison officer with *Crime Watch*. There will be a section on the next TV programme and his name will go public."

"Won't that alert him?" I felt concerned.

"He's wounded and cornered. Holed up heavens know where. We have to flush him out."

I replied bitterly, "So we now have motivation. A child molester hell-bent on revenge. All those years stuck in a cell, mostly in solitary, his hate festering away producing a toxic mix as volatile as nitro-glycerine."

Jill looked concerned. "Do you think your family need to be placed in a safe house or at least have police protection until we catch him?"

"I don't think Judy will be happy going into hiding. It would make the danger seem too real and I guess she wouldn't be too happy with a uniform at the front door. I'm staying at the house. With the Baskerville hound as a new lodger, we should be okay."

"I've had an alarm button fixed at the house linked directly to the station, we can't be too careful."

"I thought I was the one who is paranoid?"

"We're dealing with a psychopath, Tony." Jill swallowed hard. "He casts a large shadow and I don't think any of us are safe."

"Evil deeds are like fires, they can be hidden for a short time, but the smoke can't. We'll catch this madman, I promise and then we can all sleep safely in our beds."

"I hope you are right."

I took a long sip of my coffee and looked around. "Did you know I used to come here as a teenager? It felt all grown-up to drink coffee; no drugs for us kids then."

Jill smiled, "I thought we should meet here, keep out of Webster's hair and not use the station canteen."

Putting my elbow on the table and nesting my chin into the palm of my hand I muttered, "Do you know, in America they don't have police canteens. They encourage the police to sit in local diners, to be seen by the public, to be visible." I grumbled, "In this town I've got more chance of seeing a polar bear walk down Fowler Street than see a uniformed policeman."

"Well, that's America for you."

"If I was Home Secretary, I'd banish all police canteens; make our police walk the streets more."

Jill retorted, "I've got more chance to see two polar bears walking hand in hand down Fowler Street than you have of becoming Home Secretary." She paused then, shrugging, said,"Perhaps, our police keep a low profile because the public don't show them any respect."

I looked her in the eye. "How can you earn respect if you stay hidden in panda cars and police stations?"

Shot shot back, "You're starting to sound like a grumpy old man."

It was my turn to shrug, "Perhaps that's what I am."

Jill paused as she scratched the top of her lip. She said quietly, "Listen Tony, talking about showing respect, can you do me a favour?"

"What?"

"I need you to promise." She played with a packet of sugar.

"What?" I lifted up my hands in a gesture of solidarity.

She replied reluctantly, "I need you to show some respect to DC Sweetman."

Frowning, I asked, "What have I done?"

"You've done nothing, it's just your body language is always negative when he's around."

I shook my head slowly. "I didn't realise." I gave a thin smile as I grilled her, "You're not sweet on him are you?"

Jill put her head to one side and gave me her 'you've got to be kidding' look. "He's a bit young for me."

"Oh, I remember, you like the older man."

"I'm not liking anything at the moment." Jill blurted out, "Peter has gone through a divorce, the curse of our profession. He has a young daughter, Zoe, who's just started school. He's a good colleague and no doubt he'll go far. Also in a strange way," she pointed with her chin, "he reminds me of a younger version of you."

I said incredulously, "Don't know what you've got in your coffee, but it's making your mind go like mush." I sat back in the seat and paused before indicating with an open hand. "Tell me something about young DC Sweetman that reminds you of me." I crossed my arms over my chest as I waited for an answer.

She replied instantly, "He's a bloody good detective, very resilient and he likes history, especially World War One."

My eyebrows rose and I sounded surprised. "Okay, didn't know that." I didn't even know Jill knew about my interests. The thought passed through my head that she might have a file on me. Without enthusiasm,

I replied, "Okay here's the deal: I'll improve my body language and not offend the lad, okay?"

"Okay and don't call him a lad." Jill opened her handbag and taking a mirror checked her lipstick. She put her head to one side and gave me a girly look as she snapped the bag shut. "This meeting is officially over. Now Mr Bell, should we go somewhere else for something stronger to drink?"

Smiling, I replied, "I thought you'd never ask, Ms Adams."

"Allan's having a party this weekend. He's invited me." Jack turned to his mother. "Will it be okay if I go?"

The three of us were sitting in the kitchen. I was reading a book and Judy nursed a cup of tea. The dog was asleep in his basket. Judy looked at me for guidance. The dinner dishes were still piled in the sink and the central heating came on, warming the room.

I asked, "Who is Allan?"

"A kid from school, we play on the same football team." Jack stretched back on his chair. "Don't worry Granddad; there will be no drugs, I promise. Allan's parents are very strict."

Judy responded, "Didn't stop you eating too much at his birthday party. Made yourself sick, if I remember."

"Come on Mum, I was eight," replied Jack defensively. "Which eight year old doesn't stuff himself with goodies?"

I asked, "How can you be sure there'll be no drugs?"

"The local dealer, the guy with the Harley, he seems to have disappeared."

So my intervention had worked, that was good news. I cleared my throat. "That's interesting but what about drink?"

Jack smiled. "I remember a few years ago, Granddad, you told me as a youth you once got so drunk you couldn't remember where you lived, and the police brought you back home and your mum told you off for drinking under age."

I frowned and said in an indignant voice, "I told you that story?"

"Yes you did." Jack chuckled.

"And you remembered it, after all this time?" I scratched my head.

Jack said triumphantly, "I promise I won't be drinking as much as you did when you were sixteen."

I retorted, "Did I tell you the story I never broke a curfew, ever?"

Jack smirked as he shook his head lazily.

Judy said, "Jack, we want things to be normal as possible, but our lives are not normal. The man whose eye you took out is still around. We can't be too careful."

Jack looked at me, his eyes pleading. I said slowly, "Your mum is right. Here's the deal, provided your mum agrees. You can go to the party, have one drink and at eleven-thirty, I'll pick you up, I don't want you wondering around the streets at that time of night. Is that okay, Judy?"

I've lost one angel," answered Judy, "and I don't want to lose another." She snorted, "But I also don't want this one-eyed monster to ruin our lives. If Granddad thinks it's okay, I guess it'll be all right."

Jack pushed his luck. "Couldn't make it midnight, could you?"

Judy and I shared a quick raising of our eyebrows as we said in unison, "NO!"

I was through another thirty pages of my book, when I smelled the dog.

"Has the dog been out?"

Judy replied, "Yes, I took him out at five."

"Did he do his business?"

"He didn't want to."

"I think he wants to now." I looked out the window the sun was just down and the dusk was casting shadows around the houses. "I'll take him."

I started to stand but Jack beat me to it. "I'll do it, Granddad, I don't mind."

"It's getting dark, Jack." I sounded uneasy.

"I'll only be five minutes, don't worry. Besides, I think Sacha prefers me to you." He gave me a reassuring look.

Shrugging I replied, "Really?"

"Pack leader and all that." Jack already had his anorak on and slipped the dog's lead onto it. "I'll be no more than five minutes."

Then the two of them were gone.

Judy put the kettle on to kill time. After fifteen minutes I started putting on my coat. I said, "Stupid kid, he'll have met some pals. What is it about the new generation? I'm sure I wasn't like this when I was his age."

Walking down the hall I opened the front door. What I saw made my blood run cold. Limping slowly down the path, ears and tail down and his eyes swollen, was the dog. I ran to him, Judy was behind me. She screamed, "Where's my son, where's Jack?"

I stamped my foot hard on my action pedal and spoke fast. "We'll quickly check the dog first and then look for Jack." I looked at the dog. He'd been vomiting and his gums were grey. I snapped, "I think he's been poisoned." I picked up the sick animal, rushed back into the house and laid him on the kitchen table. I could hear my daughter gasping, holding back the sobs. I barked, "Get a cup of Lucozade down him, we need to make the dog vomit and get rid of the poison. Then call a vet." Turning and heading for the door, I said urgently, "I'll find Jack."

Leaving Judy in a vacuum of uncertainty, I was moving through the hallway when the telephone rang. Snatching the phone, I shouted, "Yes?"

His voice was like toxic slime oozing down the line. "Hello, Tony, Jack will be safe provided you don't call the police."

My blood froze as my legs gave way. I put a hand on the wall to keep my balance, snarling, "You son-of-a-bitch…"

"Now Tony Bell, no need for that sort of language, it's YOU I want, not your grandson." Monk's cruel laughter echoed down the line. "I'll call you back in the morning; tell you how to find him. But remember, call the cops and poor Jack's brown bread." He paused before whispering, "Have a good night, Tony."

Chapter Thirty

*S*hared history is the sweet pleasure of mutual memories and experiences that bond people together. It's the glue that binds families and fosters friendships. My memory is a wonderful treasure chest packed with my favourite things, so that when I stroll down memory lane I always end up in a happy place. Memory is not nostalgia; that's the thing which reminds you of the pleasure of sitting in front of a large fire without remembering you had to chop the wood. No memory is your autobiography that resides on a bookshelf in the library of your mind. My autobiography is not large, but it bursts with bliss and contentment, with full luminous colour you can almost touch and as I've discovered, death cannot steal your memories.

I remember: my first doll's pram; my first day at school; my first handstand; the first time I juggled three balls; the first time I put on my Brownies uniform; my first pizza; my first ice lolly; the first shoes I was allowed to choose; the first time I went on an ice rink and the first time my mum said I was *pretty. I remember each one was a stepping-stone through the dangerous rapids of that thing called life. Granddad used to joke, "Life is like a camel; it just won't back up." Granddad is funny, he was always teaching me things about how to behave in certain situations. 'Life skills' he would call it. "The only good thing about being old," he would say, "is the pleasure of handing down your wisdom to the next generation." I loved Granddad's lessons. Jack, on the other hand, was always resistant.*

I think it's that boy thing again.

Granddad taught me how to enhance your memory skills; it's called the art of mnemonics. "Mnemonics," he would say, "has a silent M to remind you it's all about memory." Let me tell you how it works. Take the camel I mentioned, the one that won't back up; there are two types of camel, the dromedary and the Bactrian. Which one has the one hump and which has the two humps? My granddad said the easy way to remember was to turn the first letter on its side and get the answer. The D on its side is one hump, (Dromedary) and the B on its side has two humps, (Bactrian). That's how the art of mnemonics work. Want to know how many days there are in any given month? No need to remember the silly poem taught by teachers; just count your knuckles, making January the first knuckle on your left hand, February being the dip in between the two knuckles. Continue around your two hands and each month that falls on a knuckle has thirty-one days. Let's think of something obscure. Do you want to know how high Mount Fuji is in Japan? Think how many days there are in a year; the answer is three hundred and sixty-five. Add the months, twelve, and you have three hundred and seventy-seven. Add a nought and that's how high Mount Fuji is in metres,

(3770m) As Granddad promised me, I promise you you'll never forget that fact. That's the art of mnemonics.

I love my memories; they are snap shots of happy times. Since I died I have one burning memory of a promise I made and there's nothing as powerful as a promise. I pledged I will kill the monster and I have no intention of breaking it. I want him to die the most horrible of deaths. He deserves it.

The monster's van runs on diesel. At the farm he has a large tank of pink tractor fuel that he uses to top up the van. He's planning to travel and he has the determined look of a man on a mission.

Mr Haines, when teaching us religious education, once told our class about Armageddon, the final biblical battle between good and evil. The good book states the beast will be killed and burnt in a lake of fire burning with brimstone. I have the feeling my own mini-Armageddon is not too far away. I have to kill the beast and burn him so badly I totally destroy his evil spirit, so that nothing will remain of him on this earth.

I think the monster is not the only one on a mission.

I watch the killer as he takes the poisoned chocolate from the fridge. Getting into his van with an assertive swagger, he drives off. I watch him again as later he parks in the shadows of a street I recognise. The street is not far from my home and I fear for my family.

My fear intensifies when I see my brother come out of the house with the new dog on a short lead. I shout at Jack about the danger, but he can't hear me, not even deep in his mind. He's too full of exhilaration, chatting to the dog, Jack is excited, his brain full of static; he's having fun as he takes the dog to a nearby park. Under the branches of an oak tree, Jack lets the dog off the lead and takes a tennis ball from his pocket. He throws the ball and as the dog chases it. The white van starts up and slowly moves towards them.

The dog returns the ball and with its tail wagging, drops it at Jack's feet. Bending down, Jack throws the ball again. The dog chases it as the van accelerates towards the tennis ball. Before Sacha reaches the yellow ball an arm comes out of the open window of the van.

"Here boy," the monster throws the chocolate towards the dog.

Jack screams, "No!" as he runs towards Sacha. But he's too late; the dog finds the chocolate and is already eating the poisoned treat. By the time Jack reaches the poor animal, Sacha is whooping in an attempt to vomit. My brother drops beside the sick animal and cradles its head. Suddenly the two of them are covered in a beam of light as the van now hurtles towards them.

I scream, "Run!"

There was no need to shout, Jack was on his feet, sprinting into the darkness of the park. I watch with horror as the white van follows him, bouncing its way across the grass.

The speeding van is almost touching Jack's legs as he throws himself to the side. It's the edge of the playing field and Jack tumbles and rolls down a slight slope onto a concrete path. The van can't follow him down the slope as the path is too narrow, and the high wire fence of tennis courts runs along the side. The van turns and drives alongside Jack on the upper side of the field. Jack finds a door in the fence and runs into the tennis courts. They are as dark as a ghost train tunnel. The van can't follow him here. He sprints across the courts; hurdling over a net he skims up the tall mesh fence on the far side like a monkey. Panting, Jack throws his legs over the wire and falls down on the other side.

Has he lost the monster?

Jack, his heart racing, takes a breather then goes into the undergrowth; he believes if he can hide, he'll be safe. Above him the moon also hides behind thick clouds.

The monster parks his van and is now on foot wearing night goggles.

Jack doesn't know the monster can see in the dark so crouches on all fours, trying not to make too much noise and give his position away.

The monster smiles triumphantly as he moves through the undergrowth stealthily; it's a game to him and he knows he'll win.

Jack screams as he feels strong arms around him and as his hope drains away a voice whispers, "Very clever," feigning admiration. Jack struggles; he's a big lad and strong, but not as powerful as his predator.

A rag is stuffed into my brother's mouth and soon he succumbs to the chemicals and falls like a dead weight, unconscious.

I watch as the monster carries my brother to his van and drives away. Later, he stops at a phone box and calls my home. I hear the monster hissing down the phone like a snake. Fighting hysteria, I hear him make a triumphant cackle as he replaces the phone. I burst into tears and sob like I've never sobbed before when minutes later, the white van drives off with my brother lying prostrate in the back. The clouds move, revealing the blue light of the moon, shining down, like some magical essence.

"Don't worry, Jack," I whispered. "Granddad will save you."

The words fade away on the wind and I'm not sure if I believe it myself.

Chapter Thirty-One

A tired-looking vet came around less than an hour later. He gave the dog an injection and left some pills. Judy looked like a ghost, her breath coming in gasps. It was a nightmare with no sense of relief. Something dreadful had happened and we both looked tormented. The vet, thank goodness, was too professional to ask any questions. The night dragged and Judy went from hysteria to total exhaustion. I resisted the urge to have a drink, wanting my head to be clear when Monk called. He would use Jack as bait, so I convinced myself my grandson would be safe for the time being.

The call came at nine in the morning. I snatched the phone off its cradle.

I heard his voice, mocking, "How are you, Tony? Had a good night?"

Ignoring my headache, I snarled, "How's Jack?"

His voice was calm. "Oh, Jack, he's dead."

I gasped and couldn't catch my breath.

He waited a minute then chuckled. "Don't worry, Tony, I'm just pulling your chain. The boy's a little bruised, but he's okay. I told you, it's you I want."

I took a deep breath. "So when do we meet?"

"It's up to you."

"Where do we meet?"

"You're the detective. Work it out, you already know."

"What do you mean?"

"You have to find me; you have less than an hour."

"And if I don't?"

"I'll kill your grandson. Goodbye, Tony."

The line went dead.

Judy was behind me in the hallway, sobbing.

I turned to her, "It'll be all right, Judy, I promise."

"Where's Jack? Where's my baby?" My daughter looked alarmed, mouth open, eyes red from crying.

"He's nearby, I think. Monk's given me an hour to figure it out, so he can't be too far away."

Judy stuttered, "What did he say?"

"He said, I already know where he's got Jack."

"What does that mean?"

"It means I've already seen the place or…" I paused, as the metaphorical penny dropped into the slot. I almost shouted, "The bastard's got Jack in the same place he held Ellie captive. The old dock."

"Oh, my God, are you going to call the police?"

"No, give me an hour; then call Jill on her direct number. Tell her everything and where I am."

"Should you take a knife, from the kitchen?"

The thought was enticing but I replied, "No, best if I don't."

"What's your plan?"

I gave Judy a weary look. "I don't have one."

It took me a while to reach the dock. I drove with due care and attention, slowly driving the car and at the same time, slowing down my speeding heart. I took deep slow breaths; I didn't want to arrive in a state of anxiety. I heard Judy's voice in my head, 'what's your plan?' What sort of man goes to war with no plan? Yet I didn't have any idea of what I'd do when I arrived. No plan, no plan. Bloody hell, it seemed Monk held all the cards.

Think Tony; what is your prime goal?

Answer: Save Jack.

That's my plan, save Jack, even if I die in achieving it. I realised I didn't care if I died; it was no big deal as long as I saved Jack, my grandson. I realised I would have to kill Monk to achieve my goal. No big deal: one dead slime ball to save a child. The speed on my speedometer was below twenty, but my knuckles on the steering wheel were white.

I parked on a double yellow line and walked towards the tall dock gates.

The Victorian gildings of the tall iron gates were covered in rust. The gates themselves were ajar and I squeezed my body through the gap without making a noise. Two fat, dirty grey pigeons on a tin roof watched me sneak across the yard and a large rat ran across my path. I found an emergency door to the warehouse and entered into the empty, cathedral-sized space of the building. I saw Monk immediately; he was down at the far end, watching me like a hawk. He seemed pleased I had arrived, no doubt a by-product of his insanity.

He looked dangerous and surely was. Like a champion boxer, watching his lesser opponent enter the arena, he oozed confidence.

I slowly walked towards him, taking in the features of the environment. This was the killing ground and every detail, no matter how small might help me survive. I moved with caution, as if walking through a minefield.

Ahead of me stood Monk, glaring like a mad Cyclops, knife in hand. Next to him was a chair which held Jack strapped to the frame. The boy had a gag over his mouth, his face was white and his eyes bulged with fear. His anorak lay on the floor next to some empty take-away food cartons.

To the right was an inspection pit and above various chains and hooks were suspended from the ceiling. To the left was the wooden hut, its door wide open. On the other side of the pit I could see a metal rod lying on the floor. It was too far away, but if reached, could be used as a weapon.

Monk was dressed in black tracksuit bottoms and wore a white vest. I could see his fit and well-trained physique. His commando tattoo was stretched over large, tight muscle and he carried no excess fat. He looked like he was still in his prime.

When I was about twenty yards away, he raised his hand.

"That's far enough, Tony. So you found me, I always knew you were a good detective."

"Let the boy go, this is between you and me."

"No it's not, Tony. It's between me and Jack Peach's entire family. You're the one who wasn't invited to the party."

"Let the boy go and I'll let you walk out of here."

Monk scratched his head, "Who are you kidding, Tony? One of us has to die and guess what?" He pointed at me with his commando dagger, "I nominate you." He gave his evil cackle again.

I shouted, "The boy's got nothing to do with what happened to you. His father is dead; you've had your revenge."

He sneered, "What about 'an eye for an eye', isn't that what the Bible tells us?" He placed the point of his dagger next to Jack's left eye. The point cut his skin and a thin tear of blood ran down his face.

I yelled, "No!" I wanted to move forward but couldn't, any attempt and Jack would be killed.

He called, mockingly, "What, you're unable to move, Tony? Tell you what, I'm going to cut out young Jack's eye and you're going to watch. Of course, you'll be unable to stop yourself and you'll attack me, which is when I will kill you. Then I'll kill Jack and I'll take an eye each from you and go and see your daughter, Judy. I'll show her the trophies, might even make her swallow them whilst I rape her before cutting her throat. Does that sound like a plan, Tony?"

I screamed, "You're sick, fucking sick!"

He screamed back, "Of course I'm sick, that's what thirteen years in solitude does to you! You can thank your son-in-law for that."

Jack was hyperventilating and I felt stunned. What to do? All my training meant nothing, because nothing in my life had prepared me for this.

Monk lifted up his knife and immediately an intense purple light illuminated behind him. I assumed I was stressing out, my eyes playing tricks. The knife was at its highest, when Monk snarled and his hand twisted back in a sort of contortion, as if he was having a muscular spasm. A look of surprise flashed over his face as the dagger jerked out of his hand and fell to the floor.

An opportunity! I found myself sprinting towards him, but Monk quickly bent down to pick up the knife and stumbled, kicking the dagger away from his feet. The knife travelled ten feet across the concrete floor and I found myself changing direction, now running towards the weapon, which seemed to be equal distance from the two of us. Monk moved like a panther and it was obvious he was going to reach the dagger first. He beat me by about three feet, but didn't have the time to pick it up, so instead he kicked it again, this time really hard. Spinning once, the knife flew through the air and went straight through the open doors of the wooden hut.

As it hit the floor I hit Monk with a flying tackle.

The two of us bundled together and crashed to the floor. As we landed heavily with me on top, Monk punched me hard in the side of the ribs. His fist felt like a mallet and I felt a rib snapping, scratching my lung. I screeched with pain, but held on. This was my only chance; I poked a finger towards his one eye. His head moved and I missed and before I could withdraw, his teeth were around my digit like a vice. He bit through flesh and blood until the bone crunched and my finger broke. Agony screamed from my lungs, it was like being attacked by a wild animal.

Suddenly he was on top landing another fist into my broken rib. A kaleidoscope of colours exploded in my brain, as I felt myself retch. My body was going into shock wanting to fall into unconsciousness and sweat oozed out of every pore.

Still I wouldn't give up; I screamed like a banshee and hit him in the throat. He gasped and butted me with his head. I felt blood gush from my nose. The man didn't seem to have an Achilles' heel; there was no vulnerability. He was an indestructible fighting machine. I was injured, fighting a younger warrior but I couldn't lose. There was too much at stake with young Jack's life.

I shot the flat of my hand upwards, like a rocket under his jaw, snapping shut his mouth. Blood gushed out with a piece of his tongue; his head shot up and he bellowed like a bull. It was the respite I was looking for, I punched him again in the throat and rolled my body over. I sprang free and was on my feet as adrenalin dampened down my pain. But Monk was also on his feet.

He spat out more blood. "Not bad for an old man, looks like I'll have to cut your head off in order to kill you."

He moved towards me in a martial art stance, he kicked his right foot out and I managed to block it, but wasn't ready for his next move. He spun around on his other foot so his back was to me, but his head spun in the opposite direction so his eyes never left mine. His right leg came up in a reverse kick. His foot caught me in the groin and I flew back three feet onto my back, leaving my wind behind.

As I gasped, he turned and ran towards the hut; wanting to retrieve his dagger. He hesitated at the door as I struggled onto one knee. He turned around to see if he had time to get the knife before I was back on my feet. Realising he did, he turned his head towards the interior of the shed.

Then it happened.

He stumbled as he went headfirst into the hut. As his body hit the floor, I held my rib and ran, crab fashion, through the pain barrier towards the shed. I slammed shut the door and dropped the wooden beam across the U bolts.

What the fuck, I had my man!

Monk, the mad monk, Rasputin, the murderer was trapped inside and my only victory ceremony was to bend over and vomit on the floor. Then as an encore I was sick again before falling onto my knees. I had won but my body felt I was defeated. Pain came from every muscle and bruising erupted over my body like mini volcanoes. The thought went through my head, 'I need a holiday'.

After I stopped retching I limped over and released Jack who immediately hugged me, reminding me of all my injuries.

I gasped out, "Aaaagh, bloody hell son, that hurts."

"Sorry Granddad." Despite it being funny, neither of us laughed.

I asked him, "Are you okay, Jack?"

"Yes, are you all right Granddad?"

"I feel like I've been run over by a steamroller, but I'll live. We've got the bastard, Jack, the nightmare is finally over."

"You were good, Granddad, like Rambo."

"I'm not sure if that's true, but thanks anyway, son."

I heard footsteps and looking up saw Jill, Judy and Sweetman running down the warehouse towards us.

Judy shouted to her son, "Are you all right, Jack?" Her words echoed around the spacious building as he fell into her arms sobbing.

Jill said, "Jeezus, Tony, looks like you've been in a plane crash."

Judy looked over her son's shoulder, "Dad, you look as if you've been running with the bulls at Pamplona and you didn't run fast enough." She sounded nervous. "Are you sure you're okay?"

I nodded, although my head felt it might fall off at any moment. She was right of course, I was getting too old to run with bulls or fist fight with a psycho.

Sweetman, ever focused, butted in, "Monk?"

I was starting to like the young DC; perhaps he was a bit like me. Still holding my rib, I indicated towards the hut, "He's in the garden shed and he's not potting geraniums."

Jill turned to Sweetman and said urgently, "Call the station, I want six uniforms down here, when we drag the scum out. I don't want any mistakes. Shackle his feet as well as his hands."

Sweetman replied, "Gotcha." He then corrected himself as he nodded his head, "Yes, mam."

Judy asked, "What's that smell?"

A thought trickled through my brain, 'why is it women have a better sense of smell than men?'

We all heard a howl coming from the shed, a haunted yell that sounded like an animal being castrated.

Jill retorted, "What the…? I think its petrol," she pointed, "and it's coming from the…"

Her last word was lost in the explosion.

As the hut blew up an inferno engulfed it. The heat was intense and we were in danger of being scorched. We retreated quickly, covering our faces with our hands. I felt my hair singeing in the heat. The wood of the hut was old, and the blistering flames quickly demolished it and everything in it. The fire licked the metal roof of the warehouse, but it didn't seem to be in danger of igniting. Black smoke billowed before escaping through a hole in the ceiling and the smell of burning flesh filled the warehouse. With eyes consumed with horror we watched the raging inferno. From the blazing shed the howling continued before eventually dying out.

Jack yelled frantically, "Burn, you bastard, burn!"

I put my arms around his shoulder, "It's okay, Jack. He's gone, Jack, gone from our lives for ever."

Judy put her hand to her mouth. "Is it over?"

I answered my daughter with a hug. "Yes, it's over."

By the time we had the fire under control there was hardly anything of Monk or the shed left. Cremated and gone; if he was lucky he might be in hell burning again. All that was left of Monk was a badly burnt foot in an incinerated boot.

Coughing to clear my lungs of smoke, I pointed to the footwear. "The bastard's definitely killed himself."

Judy fought back the tears as she said, "Don't swear Dad."

DS Jill looked at the burnt ruins. "At least it'll save the tax payer some money. No court case and no custodial sentence."

We turned and headed for the exit. We were still stunned, almost in shock, but as we made our way out, I couldn't help notice young Jack had a shadow of a smile on his lips.

Chapter Thirty-Two

I saw the fear in my brother's eyes as the monster secured him to the chair in the warehouse.

I screamed, "Don't touch my brother," but they couldn't hear me, of course.

The monster sneered as he put a gag around Jack's mouth. "You're the bait, shit brains, the bait to catch an old pike. I believe you're a fisherman, so you'll understand." He put his good eye next to jack's and snarled, "Later I'm going to cut out your eye and then kill your granddad and after I've killed you I'm gonna kill your mom." He spat on the ground. "I'm going out now, won't be long. Gonna get a Chinese because I need my strength for the big fight tomorrow. You're lucky Jack," he nodded his head. "You're going to have a ringside seat."

A sense of panic overtook me and I needed to slow down my emotions, to pause for a moment gathering my thoughts and keeping some sort of clear mind.

The monster slunk away for his Chinese take-away. Jack was secured tightly and had no chance of a breakout. Things didn't look too good for him, he struggled with his ropes, but realised there was no escaping. The look of frustration and being thwarted faded as a scared Jack closed his eyes and fell into some sort of shallow faint. He looked cold and hurt and I felt sorry for him.

The sight of my brother trussed up by the monster made me determined to help and my mind was working feverishly. How could I help? I was only a young girl who also happened to be dead. What could I do? I felt powerless as I looked around, searching for inspiration, when I saw Jack's anorak on the floor. Could it be possible? I went behind him and searched his anorak's pockets.

Please, please, please!

YES, YES, YES! It was there! How absolutely and completely awesome, thanks Jack! I found what I was looking for in an inner pocket.

I carried the object with two hands like a trophy to the hut. At the door, I hesitated; this was where I'd been held prisoner. I had to be ever so brave, so I took a deep breath and entered, hiding the object on a shelf. Granddad once taught me the best plans are not always those where people plan from the front and work things out in their heads first. Better plans are those were you start with the end result, with what success looks like and then you work backwards. My plan was the latter; I knew what success would look like, it was Armageddon, the killing of a beast. I just had to work out what the critical steps were to achieving it.

First step, I decided, was to leave the shed door open.

Despite my plan, my confidence level remained low. I was only a girl; would my idea work?

Granddad arrived the next morning. He looked like he hadn't slept for a month. He hadn't shaved and black rings surrounded his eyes. He looked older and I was afraid for him.

Granddad walked gingerly through the warehouse towards the monster. When he was the length of a net-ball pitch away the monster raised his hand.

"That's far enough, Tony. So you found me, I always knew you were a good detective."

Granddad yelled back, "Let the boy go, this is between you and me."

I shouted too. "Yes, let my brother go."

The monster said to Granddad, "No it's not, Tony. It's between me and Jack Peach's entire family. You're the one who wasn't invited to the party."

"Let the boy go and I'll let you walk out of here."

I shouted again. "Yes, otherwise you'll be really sorry!"

The monster scratched his head, "Who are you kidding, Tony? One of us has to die. Guess what? I nominate you." He gave his evil cackle again.

"The boy's got nothing to do with what happened to you." Granddad pleaded, "His father is dead; you've had your revenge."

The horrible monster mocked, "What about 'an eye for an eye', isn't that what the Bible tells us?" He placed the point of his dagger on Jack's face. The point cut Jack's skin and a thin line of blood oozed out.

I turned to Granddad. "Save my brother, Granddad. Do something!"

"No!" He looked petrified.

"What, you're unable to move, Tony? Tell you what, I'm going to cut out young Jack's eye, you're going to watch. Of

course you'll be unable to stop yourself and you'll attack me, which is when I'll kill you. Then I'll kill Jack and I'll take an eye each from you and go and see your daughter, Judy. I'll show her the trophies, might even make her swallow them whilst I rape her before cutting her throat. Does that sound like a plan, Tony?"

Granddad screamed, "You're sick, fucking sick!"

I didn't like to hear Granddad swear, but I couldn't help agreeing. I yelled at the monster, "Yes, you're sick!"

"Of course I'm sick, that's what thirteen years in solitude does to you! You can thank your son-in-law for that."

I'd heard enough. It was time for action. Taking a deep breath, I raced towards the monster. As he raised the knife high into the air, I finished my run in front of him. An intense purple flash occurred as I quickly raised my left arm, putting it horizontal across the killer's wrist. I then brought my right hand behind his arm and caught hold of my other hand. I now had a fulcrum and with minimum pressure I pushed my left arm, forcing the dagger from his hand. This was a move my granddad taught me. He said it was an old oriental trick, invented by monks who were not allowed to carry weapons.

Wow, it worked! Awesome, Granddad!

The monster had a surprised look on his face as the knife jerked out of his hand and fell towards the floor. On impact I kicked the weapon and it flew across the floor. I was now putting my plan into action. Both Granddad and the monster were now running to the knife, but I didn't want either of them to get it. I was at the knife first. Like a penalty kick, my foot caught the knife and launched it through the air, spinning it once. The knife headed towards the open door of the hut and

241

disappeared inside. I jumped up, punching the air as I shouted, "Goal!"

Granddad and the monster were now fighting like two wild dogs. Granddad looked like he had all the breath knocked out of his body, he looked disoriented and the monster was winning the contest. The killer did a sort of mule kick that sent poor Granddad flat on his bottom.

I shouted at the monster, "Get the knife!" I don't know if he heard deep in his brain, but he turned and ran towards the hut. At the door he hesitated, wondering if he had time to get the dagger. He looked over his shoulder. Granddad, despite being winded was getting up on his feet. The monster was having second thoughts about going into the hut.

I ran at him, hands outstretched. I hit him in the small of the back, the same way he had shoved me into his van. He shot forward, falling onto the floor. My momentum also took me into the hut, my old cell, but I wasn't worried. This was part of my plan. Moments later, I heard the door slamming shut behind me as Granddad locked us in. That was part of my plan too. Granddad thought he'd only captured one person in the hut, but there were two of us. I was now trapped inside my prison cell with the monster. I watched as, dagger in hand, he got to his feet.

There he was; the filth who killed girls, who wanted to kill my family. Now it was just me and him.

I smiled; my little plan had worked perfectly. I felt really pleased with myself. Wicked! I wasn't prepared for what happened next, though. This had not been a part of my plan.

His one eye showed fear. "Who are you?"

Awesome! I'd never expected him to be able to see me! How cool is that?

Getting over my surprise I said, "It's me, Ellie."

He sneered, "Don't be daft, Ellie's dead." He forced a laugh, but it didn't sound very confident.

I smiled. Honestly, I just couldn't help it. "That's right, you killed me."

I heard him gulp as he processed the information. "I don't believe in ghosts, get out of my way, otherwise I'll have to hurt you."

The interior of the hut seemed to be draped in an amethyst light, as if there was a lamp on with a purple shade.

I said, "You can't hurt me anymore. In fact you are never going to hurt anybody ever again." Next to me stood the large jerrycan of petrol. Without taking my eyes off the monster I turned the cap slowly. With each turn, the purple light got more intense and as the light increased so my smile widened. When the cap was off I dropped it to the floor.

"What are you doing?" The monster sounded scared.

"What do you think I'm doing? Duh!"

Still smiling, I pulled the jerrycan over and as it crashed to the floor, the petrol started gushing out. I watched as the inflammable liquid soaked into the wooden floor and his tracksuit bottoms. I thought he might attack me, but fear was rooting him to the spot. He didn't want to rush at me and discover what he already suspected. I was me; the dead Ellie.

I raised my hand up to a shelf where I retrieved what I had previously hidden, the object from Jack's anorak pocket.

"What have you got there?" The fear dripped off his tongue, he was terrified and, typical of all bullies, the coward lay just below the skin.

David McLaren

I opened my hand and showed him. He gasped as I replied, "It's my dad's lighter, my brother Jack carried it in his pocket and guess what?"

"What?" The one-eyed monster was petrified and the knife fell from his grasp.

I replied, "We're going to have some fun."

I clicked the lighter and a spark was produced to a sound of a howl as the monster wailed with absolute terror. There followed an almighty explosion as the petrol fumes ignited and exploded into an apocalypse that took the roof off. Fear twisted his features as flames licked and danced up his body. The monster was like a Guy Fawkes dummy, a pyre of flesh curling like burnt bacon. His remaining eye seemed to melt. I watched and of course the flames couldn't harm me, although my sense of smell was intact. I could smell his flesh burning, the stink of his rotten body ablaze overpowering the smell of petrol. I watched with satisfaction as he turned charcoal then ash black. It took a long time for him to die and he screamed throughout his roasting. His remains were eventually reduced to a pile of hot cinders on the ground with only a boot and bits of a foot left behind. I pondered on whether the monster would spend eternity limping around the abyss that is hell wondering where his foot was.

The monster was dead. I'd killed him, just like I'd promised and as my Granddad had told me many times, there's nothing as powerful as a promise. The burnt foot proved justice had been served.

My lovely granddad once taught me, justice is the key that unlocks the door of resentment and the handcuffs of hate. Justice is also the power that breaks the chains of bitterness and frees

244

you from the shackles of sorrow. When he'd told me I had no idea what he meant. I do now.

Armageddon and five gallons of petrol had set my family free and that made me happy.

I watched as my family and the two police people left through the old dock gate. Granddad was stooping with pain as he watched his grandson run to his car.

Jack picked something off the windscreen. Waving the object in the air, he shouted, "Granddad, you've got a parking ticket!"

They all stopped walking and started laughing, then kept laughing until they couldn't catch their breath. The laughter turned to hilarious hysterics. I laughed too, because, yes, my family were now truly free to move on with their lives.

The monster was dead, the nightmare over.

Chapter Thirty-Three

Two months later I was sitting back in the County Hotel with Jill. Winter was showing itself in icy patterns on the windows. I pitied anybody who didn't have antifreeze in their car's cooling system in this part of the world. We kept our overcoats on as the room was just above freezing and the beer was cold. A few people were sitting at other tables, but the room was far from crowded.

Jill asked, "How are you doing, Tony?"

"Had an X-ray today, seems my rib is almost back to normal." I showed her my bandaged finger, "Nearly fixed."

"Good, I'm pleased for you. How's the family?"

"Apart from the dog which still resents me, we're doing fine. Judy wants a break, a holiday."

"Don't blame her."

"She has her bad moments, who wouldn't? But Jack is remarkable, he doesn't seem at all fazed by being kidnapped by a madman and he's doing well at school."

"He's a good kid."

"Yes he is. He's going to be okay."

Jill seemed elsewhere and was silent for a while. Then she looked at me. "I went to Ellie's grave today, took some flowers."

I sounded surprised. "You didn't have to do that, but thanks anyway."

"Don't know why I did it. Just felt an impulsion. Still, I felt good after I did it."

"Ellie had that sort of power over people, could always make them feel better about themselves."

"Oh," Jill put her hand in her coat pocket. "I have something for you."

She handed me a silver cigarette lighter, I recognised it as my late son-in-law's. "Where did you get it?"

"It was found in the ashes of the fire, must have been the source of ignition when Monk killed himself."

I looked at the object, which was in pristine condition. "It seems to have survived the fire very well."

"Yes, that's what we thought. Any ideas?"

"What? You mean how it survived the fire?"

"Yes."

I shook my head very slowly, "No, just some things are beyond forensics. I'll get it back to Jack, he'll be delighted."

"You won't tell him where it was found." She sounded concerned.

"No, I'll leave that bit out. He's had enough nightmares to last him a lifetime."

Jill smiled, "Got some more news for you."

"What's that?"

"Webster's being made to take early retirement, it's only a few years early, but he's not too pleased."

"Does that mean possible promotion for you?"

She put her head slowly to one side. "I'm afraid not."

I sat back in my seat. "Not because you're a woman?"

Jill smiled again. "No, I'm taking early retirement too."

I replied incredulously, "You've got to be joking; you're too young, surely."

A thin line formed over her lips. "It's a medical retirement."

I leaned forward and touched her hand. "Bloody hell, Jill. What's wrong?"

She replied sadly, "Tinnitus; the ringing in the ears."

I burst out laughing. "Is Miss Donaldson still giving out HR advice? Tinnitus can't be disproved, bloody marvellous."

A dark look crossed Jill's face. She thundered, "Listen you silly bugger!" She tapped the table with her finger. "I really do have tinnitus, it's not bloody funny."

I kept laughing then the smile drained from my face. "Oh shit, you really do have it."

"Yes, I don't want to retire, I love my job."

I lied, "I know all about it, it's not a funny affliction."

"Fuck off, Tony. What am I going to do?"

I thought for a moment then suggested, "We could go into partnership. What about pet detectives?"

"What?" It was Jill's turn to look incredulous.

"Pet detectives: we look for lost animals, find them and overcharge the delighted owners."

"I don't think so and don't suggest a private detective agency, either."

I shrugged. "Gosh, this town already has enough fish and chip shops, I've got no idea."

"What about travel partners?"

There was silence for a few moments. "You're kidding, right?"

Jill shook her head.

"Okay, you need to explain a little bit more."

She shrugged. "No, I'm not kidding, we're both retired, let's travel together. See the world."

"Wow, that's from the left field, as our American friends would say."

"Well, let's keep the American metaphors coming; are you going to 'step up to the plate'?"

I was in a state of shock. Beer night was turning into a life- changing experience. I stuttered, "Sounds okay, but have you really thought this through?"

"Of course I have. We like each other, don't we?"

I replied honestly, "You're my best friend, Jill."

"I am?" Jill smiled with relief.

"Yes, I guess you are. Hadn't thought about it until now, but you are my best friend."

"That's great, Tony. You're my best friend too. Have you ever been to Marrakesh?"

"No, but I have always wanted to go."

"Great, I've bought two airline tickets for February. One's in your name."

"Bloody hell, lass, you don't waste time, do you? Separate rooms I hope."

"Couldn't afford two rooms, one shared room; two beds. Don't worry, Tony, you've got nothing I haven't seen before."

"You do know I snore?"

"Tony, sweetheart, all men snore, it's something we women have to put up with."

"Are you sure I'm not too old for you?"

She pointed a finger at me and said in a threatening manner, "I'm forty-eight. If you ever ask that question again I'll do to you what I did to my first aggressive coke-head arrest."

"Oh, what's that?"

"Let's just say he still speaks with a soprano voice."

"Oh, I get it."

Jill took a drink, dabbed her lips with a small handkerchief and said, "You can now buy me dinner."

"What?"

"You can buy me dinner. No Indian, must be Italian, there's a nice restaurant at the Old Custom's House." I looked puzzled as she continued, "Look, I bought you the tickets, only fair you buy dinner."

"Bloody hell, it's just as well I haven't eaten yet." I wasn't sure how phoney my surprise was.

Jill retorted, "No wonder they called you Ding Dong Bell."

I leaned forward and demanded, "Who called me Ding Dong Bell?"

She laughed, "They all did. Ding Dong Bell!"

"Bloody hell, I never knew." I shook my head in disbelief.

Jill laughed harder, "I'm just joking, Tony. But later after the wine, I will tell you what your nickname really was."

I put my head to one side. "Will I be pleased?"

"Perhaps," she grinned and two dimples appeared in her cheeks. "You'll have to wait and find out."

I smiled and finished off my beer. "So you like Italian, that's good, so do I."

She raised an eyebrow. "Something else, you need to know about my culinary preferences."

"What's that?"

"The appetisers, the hors d'oeuvre are as important as the main meal to me. We mustn't ever rush the starters. I've got to be in the mood to enjoy the main meal."

"What, every time?"

There was a pause. "Well not necessarily. Occasionally, very occasionally, if I'm really hungry, we can go straight to the main course, but I usually need to drink a bottle of wine first."

I frowned, "Jill, we are talking about food, aren't we?"

She leaned over and kissed me on the cheek. Sitting back and with her eyes wide and bright she touched my hand and whispered, "Of course, Tony, of course."

The Last Chapter

*M*y name is Ellie Peach, like the fruit. My granddad would say, "twice as sweet" and I was. Now I'm dead, but not unhappy. My family aren't unhappy either; Granddad has a travel partner and they have great holidays together. I like Jill, she makes Granddad laugh, which use to be my job. Now it's Jill's, but I'm not jealous. She looks like an American movie star who use to play a detective on TV. I don't know which one, because the programme was on long before I was born, but I do know it was Granddad's favourite detective show. They are both happy and so am I.

My brother Jack has grown up into a fine man. Mum says he's just like his dad, so I can see how Dad looked. Jack didn't join the Marines, though. He became a policeman instead. When he's twenty-six, he'll marry my best friend, Talia, and they'll have three children, two girls and a boy. Jack will teach his son how to fish and they will all live happily. Mum will be a grandmother. Granddad will love the children but will hate being called Great-Grandpa.

I'm so happy for them.

Mum is very good at hiding her sadness. She tells everyone she is moving on, but it's a little white lie. On the first anniversary of my death, Mum wanted to visit Dad's grave, but the Falkland Islands are just too far away. At a loss, she decided to visit her Great Granddad's war grave in France as a substitute. Granddad wanted to take her, but she told him she wanted to visit alone.

I watched from heaven as she booked a small hotel, south of Arras in France, near the killing fields of World War I. She sat alone in the restaurant, regretting not having Granddad along. She was looking at the menu when she heard a voice.

"Mrs Peach?"

She looked up in astonishment. "DC Sweetman?"

"Actually, it's now DS Sweetman, I got a promotion. What are you doing here?"

"I'm visiting a war grave of a relative."

He looked surprised. "I thought Tony would be with you."

Mum shook her head. "No, I told Dad I wanted to be alone."

He looked apologetic. "I'm sorry, should I leave?"

Mum shook her head again. "No, now I'm here, it's actually nice to see someone I know."

He smiled and asked, "May I join you for dinner, Mrs Peach?"

She smiled. "Yes you may, but only if you call me Judy."

"In which case," *he said sitting down,* "you must call me Peter."

Mum asked, "What are you doing here?"

"Oh, I'm a history buff. I'm thinking of writing a book about the battle of the Somme. I arrived here last night. I'm booked in this hotel for a week. The owners are nice, an Englishman and his French wife."

"I'm just here for three days, just a short break. It was Ellie's anniversary a few days ago. I needed to get away."

"Perhaps I could help you find this relative's grave."

"I would like that very much, Peter." Mum looked grateful.

He smiled. "You should try the speciality of the house."

"What's that?"

"Beetroot soup, it's delicious."

They both giggled, happy to have bumped into each other. Life is full of strange encounters that change people's lives forever.

I watched with joy as my mum fell in love again. A year later they married. A happy Jack was best man and Talia and Peter's daughter, Zoe were Mum's bridesmaid. Granddad danced at his daughter's wedding. He's a great detective my granddad, but duh, a hopeless dancer. I mean he's really, really, REALLY embarrassingly bad!

So that is the future for my family. They recovered from the tragedy, but never forgot me and were able to find happiness again. What about me? Well, let me tell you.

After the monster was destroyed I found myself back in heaven. Jessica waved to me from her carousel and shouted, "The door to your heaven is open."

I wandered towards the bleak building, watching in wonder as flowers bloomed open as I passed them. The blue and gold sky had a few white clouds, all puffy and soft. A soft breeze kissed my skin and I felt full of love. As I came to the great wooden door, I could see it was ajar. With trepidation, I squeezed into the building and my eyes opened wide with what I saw. It took my breath away.

The interior was the best ICE RINK I'd ever seen.

I stepped inside and found myself skating, white skate shoes magically appearing on my feet. The sides of the rink were filled with flowers, beautiful white flowers of every kind, filling the room with their perfume. Because this is heaven, I know the flowers will never wilt.

There is also an audience, watching my every move. The rink is packed to the rafters with mohair and alpaca-plush spectators, who sit with their glass eyes and little black noses watching my every move. I recognise some of the teddy bears: Paddington, Rupert, Winnie-the-Pooh, Becky and Barnaby, Sooty, Yogi and even Mr Bean's Teddy is there. I waved to the onlookers but, of course, they can't wave back.

Meanwhile, the air is vibrating with the music of the Beach Boys' song, God Only Knows.

I freely skate with joy in my heart, and just as before when I won the competition, I can't fall, no matter how hard the jump or turn. I am going to skate for eternity and this is my heaven, my paradise.

> "If you should ever leave me,
> Though life would still go on, believe me,
> The world could show nothing to me,
> So what good would living do me?
> God only knows what I'd be without you."

A two-foot turn, a half loop, a toe loop, a salchow (WOW!) and then I'm doing an inverted spiral. Let's try a one-handed biellman with a broken leg spin. It works, how cool is this? Dimples appear in my cheek as I smile.

I'm gliding backwards, picking with the left toe and leaping off the right leg. Then I leap from a back edge of the foot and make more rotations in the air. This is wicked. As I do a double rotation, I just wish my family could see me now.

I'm in the middle of my routine when I hear a strong rich voice resonating over the ice, "Well done, Ellie."

I turn, still skating and see a man in uniform looking at me and he's clapping. I have never seen the man before, but I know who he is.

I skate and glide towards his open arms as I scream with joy, "DADDY!"

We collide in a crescendo of emotion.

You see it wasn't only my heaven, it was his too.

I'm a daddy's girl now, skating in heaven. Could my heart hold more?

Heaven only knows.

THE END

David McLaren

Acknowledgements

I started writing this book as a way of dealing with my serious health problems, and indeed it took my mind off the issue for a number of weeks. I enjoyed writing and loved the idea of having two voices. Halfway through the book I had no idea who the monster would be, so I was as surprised as the reader. Ellie started off being twelve years of age (the same age as the "real" Ellie, our granddaughter) at the beginning of the book, and I had no idea when I began she would induce the naughty dream with Adam. I hope it didn't offend any readers. Special thanks to Ariom Dahl, a very generous person who helped with the proof reading.

Special thanks also go to all my friends and granddaughters who lent me their names for the book. May I say, none of the characters are actually based on these people, (apart from Sacha the dog!) The real

Tony Bell would never head-but anybody, and to be honest he would never make a good detective, but he's not too bad at dancing!

Also thanks to the lady in Spain who helped me with my Word programme when it went all weird! Thanks to Brian Wilson and Tony Asher for the words of the song, *God Only Knows*. As the character, Ellie, would say, "Awesome!"

So if you were kind enough to buy this book, my warmest thanks. My only reward is that you enjoyed it. Also, thanks for the many people who have supported both my wife and I during the last few years.

Other Books By The Author

Saving Starfish

Hotel Le Brambily

Books the author wished he'd written:-

The Bible

David McLaren

Now read on for a taste of the author's previous novel:

Hotel Le Brambily

Everybody remembers the day President Kennedy was killed.

Phillip remembers for a different reason.

It was the day he made love to a ghost.

David McLaren

Hotel Le Brambily

Chapter One

When Jack Kennedy died, my life changed forever. Everyone alive that day, can recall the moment in 1963 when they heard about the assassination of the American President. As the news soaked like indelible ink into the collective memory, I can remember only one thing. It was the day I met and fell in love with a ghost.

Wait a minute. Having read the above you are probably thinking I should have started this book with, "Once upon a time…", because you think this is a fairy tale or make-believe. Well, let me tell you, the truth is stranger than any fiction.

Perhaps, dear reader, you have come to the conclusion I must be insane or eccentric. For the record, the only thing crazy is what happened to me.

Like all lives, mine has had its share of the mundane. Not wanting to bore you, I have only written about those extraordinary moments, which all lives have and which make them all unique. It's just that my life has had more than its share of remarkable times.

This is a story that explores the universal themes of fear and heroism. It involves passion from beyond the grave and the opportunity to change the past to make a better future. It has hope, desire and whimsy in its pages, but most of all this book is about love. My name is Phillip Joseph, named after my father who was a war hero, and this is the story of my life and the people I knew.

I hope you enjoy it.

The day JFK was shot I was twenty-three years old and a passenger in Toby Mansfield's open-top Austin Healey.

"How long will it take?" I raised my voice above the roar of the engine.

The French countryside, a vast canvas of imposing hedgerows and a skyline stabbed by tall pine trees, passed us by in a blur. Toby, who was my publisher as well as my best friend, ignored the speed limit and pressed his foot to the floor. The car had no radio, so we were unaware of the events taking place thousands of miles away in Texas.

"Takes hours, just sit back and enjoy the ride. I promise we'll be there in time for dinner."

I scraped a living writing cheap novels about a fictional spy called Jim Spencer, a poor man's James Bond with enough fans to consistently keep my books in the lower hundreds of the best-selling list, helping me pay my rent. We were heading for Toby's château in the Vendée region, which he had inherited from his late father along with a publishing firm. We had left Calais after shopping at a newly built supermarket and filling the boot with wine, cigarettes and other provisions. The pound was strong, like the wind in my face, so everything on the shelves had been incredibly cheap.

We had been as excitable as two children in a toy store.

"It's my first visit to France," I said as I scanned the countryside.

"What do you think?" Toby grinned. "My parents loved it and bought their holiday château in the mid-Fifties. They paid peanuts for it."

"I can't help thinking it looks a little familiar."

"Of course it does. It's just like England except a lot cleaner."

I turned my head towards him. "No, I mean it looks familiar, as if I've been here before."

Toby laughed out loud. "The French have a word for that, *déjà vu*. It's your creative mind, no wonder you're a writer."

I ignored the accolade because Toby, the smooth and very successful publisher, passed them out like cheap sweets. My friend planned to sell his inherited publishing firm when he turned forty in order to retire and live the millionaire's life in France.

I had no such plans.

Toby continued, "Give me a universal law."

I thought for a moment then replied slowly, "Chips always taste better off another person's plate."

Toby shook his head sadly. "I take back what I said about your creative mind."

"So you disagree?"

"No, I suppose it's correct. It's just not one of your more insightful ones, less universal, more a bye-law."

"Okay, here is another one." Pausing and gathering my thoughts, I then said, "Everybody has one day in their life when something happens and their life is changed forever. It's as if fate sticks her foot out and trips you up, and as you fall all your plans and dreams get smashed. Then destiny has to reset your compass, and your life takes a completely different course and will never be the same again."

A few minutes passed and then Toby said, "Okay, that's a little bit better. I suppose even a little profound." He then took a deep breath and with his eyes wide said, "Whenever you dial a wrong number, it's never engaged or a no reply. Some stupid bugger will always answer."

I sighed, grinned and reluctantly nodded my head all at the same time.

"Now that's what you call a universal law." Toby leaned over and laughed out loud again. He was already in the holiday mood.

We drove in silence for about three minutes when suddenly Toby's foot lurched off the accelerator as he launched his left hand into the air. "Bloody hell, do you know what we've forgotten?"

"What?"

Toby shouted, "Bloody water."

"What do you mean?"

"We forgot to buy some water at the supermarket." He grabbed the steering wheel as his foot came down hard on the pedal in an impotent attempt to squash his frustration. The rear of the car swerved a little, but held the road.

I said incredulously, "Buy water? That's ridiculous, can't we use tap water?"

"Not bloody likely. Unless you want to spend your holiday sitting on a French toilet. We're in a foreign country and need bottled water. I'll remind you of universal law number one, commonly called sod's law: You'll only ever forget something if it's important."

"Crap!"

"Exactly!"

We drove the next few kilometres in stony silence. The only sound came from the engine, which sounded like it was overdue a service. As usual, when Toby's moods cast a gloom, it was me who blew it away.

"Cheer up, Toby. We must be able to buy water on the way?"

He growled, "Another universal law, I'm afraid. Forget something you really need and it's guaranteed there will be no shops *en route*." He took a deep breath. "I have to tell you there are no more shops between here and the house. Sorry chum. I'm afraid it looks like we've made a bit of a horlicks."

"There's a T-junction up ahead, about five kilometres." I rubbed my hands as if feeling cold and my eyes narrowed as I said, "We can turn off and find somewhere."

Toby turned his head and looked at me. He had a quizzical look on his face. "How the bloody hell would you know that?"

I shrugged. "I must have seen a road sign, back there. There will probably be an inn or a *pension*. We could buy some water there." I convinced myself I had indeed seen a road sign.

After exactly five kilometres we came to the T-junction. On the side of the road stood a two-pump petrol station, the oil company's old logo faded with the sun. Toby snorted and turned the steering wheel right, taking the car onto a minor road.

I said, "Another few minutes and we'll find an inn."

For some reason, I sounded confident.

"Ah, you do have a creative mind." Toby raised one eyebrow. "I hope you can use it to find us some girls when we arrive at château Mansfield. I haven't had a bonk for weeks."

The fields on each side of the narrow road were filled with sweet corn, over ripe and desperate for harvest. Crossing another smaller road before going over a shimmering railway line, we headed down into a valley of ancient trees. As the valley floor levelled we felt the rough road turning into cobblestones. We drove into a small square and there before us stood two buildings. One, partially covered in a thick green vine, had the name Hôtel Le Brambily arched over its door.

"I told you!" The smugness of my voice matched my look of satisfaction.

Toby rolled his eyes. "Lucky guess, Phillip, nothing more."

I replied quickly, "The only sure thing about luck is that it will change." I opened the door and standing on the cobblestones removed my hat and scarf. The building in front of me seemed oddly familiar.

Toby switched off the engine and sat back, relaxing in his leather seat. He reflected for a moment before announcing triumphantly, "That's a line from *The Spy and the Girl with the Butterfly Tattoo*, chapter two, I think." He pointed at me with a finger. "You're the bloody author so you should know."

I couldn't take my eyes off the hotel as I retorted, "I know I'm surprised you took the time to read it." I threw my hat and scarf onto the back seat and wiping my lips, ignored the unexpected cold grip in my stomach.

Toby replied, "It's bad karma for a publisher not to read his own publications."

"It was chapter three actually." I took some francs from my wallet. "So how many bottles should I get?"

"Get six and make sure it's the stuff without the bubbles, all that gas makes me belch. Whilst you're doing that, I'll have a smoke and check the oil." Toby joked. "You know how I like to get my dipstick out and besides, we don't want to break down *en route*."

I left Toby and his dipstick and walked the few steps towards the hotel, the sun on my back, the cobbles a painful reminder my shoes were overdue for repair. The two-storey hotel was small, possibly no more than ten to twelve guest rooms, and the brown paintwork was flaking, exposing the ash grey wood beneath to the sun. I walked passed some tables and chairs and headed for a small door that looked as if it would lead to a bar. As I entered I remember being surprised how much colder the interior was after the warmth of the square. Behind the counter, a large man with a walrus moustache stopped cleaning a glass and stared at me, his eyes open wide.

A look of surprise covered his face like a mask. Nearby, his only customer, a tired looking *gendarme*, unshaven and aged a few years older than myself, slammed his half glass of beer onto his table. With an incredulous look on his face, the policeman wiped some froth from his top lip. His eyes were unblinking.

The room suddenly felt colder.

The barman spoke. "So you have returned."

I looked at him, convinced I had misheard. "Excuse me?"

"So you have returned, Phillip."

"You know me?" My brain went into overdrive. Obviously I looked like another customer. One who happened to also be called Phillip.

"Of course, you are Phillip Joseph. How could I not know you?"

I thought, put this in a novel and Toby would laugh it off the press.

I hesitated as lines creased on my forehead. "Have we met before?"

Behind me a table leg scraped against the floor. The *gendarme* stood up, pulled on his hat, leaving his drink unfinished and headed for the door. A look of distain twisted his bottom lip. When he opened the door I noticed Toby and his car were no longer in the square. There was only a ribbed horse and equally thin driver sitting in a trap, as it rattled noisily over the cobbles, heading back up the valley. Not for the first time my friend's impulsive nature meant he had abandoned me. As there was no girl involved, I assumed my fickle friend was heading back to the garage to purchase some desperately needed oil.

I turned towards the barman and shook my head slowly. I said in a soft voice. "I think you are mistaken."

His response was instant. "Of course, Monsieur, I must be thinking of someone else." He put down the glass and towel. He raised his voice as his face went red with fury. "Someone who marries my daughter then disappears and returns without a bye or bye and tells me I'm mistaken." He leaned his head to one side. He bellowed, "I think it is you who has made the mistake, no?"

I ignored him because I knew he was mistaken. I'd never had a girlfriend, never mind been married. Ignoring my feeling of being mystified, I insisted, "Six bottles of water, please."

"You need more than water, I think." The man's face, with its large nose hanging over his moustache, looked like a volcano ready to explode. "What you need is…"

He was interrupted by a soft, silky voice which swept through the small room.

"It's all right, father. We don't know what Phillip has been through. There has to be a good reason for his absence."

I turned and gasped. Standing by an internal doorway was a young woman in her early twenties, dressed in a plain black dress with a plunging neckline. Her dark hair hung loosely on her bare shoulders. Around her neck hung a delicate chain with a small, gold crucifix, and high on her right breast I could see the tattoo of a small butterfly. The woman was beautiful and looking at me. She smiled. Her eyes were bright and mysterious.

I stared back at her, my mouth half open. Bloody hell, it can't be!

It was the sort of reaction you would have if you bumped unexpectedly into someone famous, like a Hollywood star, except she wasn't. I experienced spooked exhilaration because she looked identical to a fictitious character I'd created. Here from the pages of my books was the lover of Jim Spencer, the girl with the butterfly tattoo. This can't be true.

"Rita?" I heard my voice, it sounded far away.

"Yes Phillip, it is Rita. You are safe now." Her voice like warm honey was intoxicating. "Welcome home, Phillip." She walked towards me and I felt her hand slip into mine. "Come, I have what you need."

I swear when she touched me I felt a jolt of electricity pass through my body. As in a dream, I followed her as we headed for a door. She was bare foot. We walked along a dark corridor before we came to a flight of spiral stairs. As we started to ascend, she stopped. Still holding my hand, she pointed at the fifth step. Turning she looked at me, putting a finger to her voluptuous lips. I instinctively knew if I stood on this step it would creak.

She whispered, "Old habits die hard, is it not so, Phillip?"

She stepped over and I did likewise as I followed her upstairs. Bewildered and bewitched, my heart pounded in my chest as we walked along a passageway. Stopping, she turned and grinned, as she used her shoulder to push open a heavy door. In the middle of the room was a large double bed with a brass headboard. We heard the loud slam of the outside door and the lock groaning as a key was turned. Rita moved to the small window and pulled back the curtains.

Looking down she said, "My father has shut up shop. He won't be back for hours. We're the only people in the hotel." She turned towards me. "As you are my husband, I suggest you ravish me."

Gliding towards me, she gently held my face and placed her lips on mine. All thoughts drained away as we kissed passionately. She expertly removed my clothes and murmured, "I've missed you."

My heart was pounding; my legs weak and my breath came in gasps. I was young; blood pumped me up and pushed aside any sense of caution I should have had. Passion rushed through me like a bush fire. I watched with wonder as her clothes fell away.

Our clothes in a heap on the floor, she took my hand and interlocking our fingers, led me to the bed. I felt the mattress give as I lay beside her.

Resting her head on the soft pillow, she turned and looked at me. Her eyes sparkled from behind thick black lashes as she whispered, "It's been a long time, Phillip."

She pulled me towards her, her body hungry for mine. Putting her hands behind my neck, she pulled me tight into her chest. As our lips met again I heard her moan and as our bodies moved together, we made passionate love. My sweat mingled with hers and soon I was unable to stop, even if I had wanted to.

I thought I'd gone to heaven.

Afterwards I fell into a deep sleep, my body sated, only to be woken a few hours later as her lips journeyed, yet again, over my body. She was kneeling on the bed beside me, naked except for the gold crucifix and chain. My hands ran over her firm body, as I explored the now familiar landscape of her body, with its secret valleys and hidden pleasures now exposed. Her scent filled the room and her fingertips caressed the folds of my skin. The sensuous enjoyment overwhelmed me, in waves it ebbed and flowed before it peaked and in its wake left a tidemark of contentment. Outside it was night and through the curtains, the full moon cast dancing shadows on the wallpaper.

"Your wound has recovered well." She traced her hand over the left side of my rib cage.

"It's a birth mark." I shrugged. The purple, bruised skin was shaped like a squashed strawberry.

She turned and looked into my eyes. "You were shot, my love. I took out the bullet myself. Have you forgotten?"

I stared at her blankly and before I could answer, she giggled and with her legs bent, sat on my hips. Her long hair fell onto my face as she bent her head and kissed my lips feverishly.

I gasped as I entered her and as our bodies moved in harmony, we made love again.

The sound of a distant church bell brought me out of my deep sleep. The height of the sun in the sky was high and I calculated it must have been mid morning. Rita was gone, leaving behind the indentation of her body on the mattress. I felt ravenous and a thirst burnt my throat. Desperate for a drink, I suddenly remembered Toby. Dressing quickly, I ran from the hotel into the square. As I crossed the cobbles, three pigeons flew from under my feet. I saw Toby asleep at the wheel of his parked car.

The words tumbled out of my mouth. "Toby, I'm so sorry." I shook his shoulder. One eye opened followed by the other. He swung his wrist up and looked at his watch.

"Bloody hell, how long does it take to get some water?"

With narrowed eyes, he looked me over like a suspicious customs officer.

"You do have the water, don't you?"

I shook my head as a pain started behind my eyes.

"Another bloody horlicks! Well jump in. Just as well you're my best friend. Otherwise I could really get hacked off."

The car kicked up dust as it headed away from the square and up the valley.

Gripping the steering wheel tight, Toby said, "Ten minutes to find out the bloody hotel didn't sell water. The village idiot would have been quicker."

Ten minutes? My headache turned into a vicious migraine.